Debrah,

Forty Years Too Late?

....

Gaylene Nunn

*Be kind to someone &
make their day!*

Gaylene Nunn

Weezie Publishing

Copyright © 2022 Gaylene Nunn

The characters and events in this book are fictitious. Any similarity to real persons, living or dead, is coincidental and not intended by the author.

No part of this book may be reproduced, or stored in a retrieval system, or transmitted in any form or by any means, electronic, mechanical, photocopying, recording, or otherwise, without express written permission of the publisher.

Library of Congress Control Number: TXu 2-325-751

Cover design by: Lynn Greenwood & Randy McCauley

Printed in the United States of America

All rights reserved.

ISBN: 9798985879926

gaylenenunn.com

Contents

Dedication	VI
Introduction	VII
1. Chapter 1	1
2. Chapter 2	4
3. Chapter 3	7
4. Chapter 4	13
5. Chapter 5	14
6. Chapter 6	19
7. Chapter 7	23
8. Chapter 8	30
9. Chapter 9	33
10. Chapter 10	38
11. Chapter 11	44
12. Chapter 12	49
13. Chapter 13	54

14. Chapter 14	60
15. Chapter 15	64
16. Chapter 16	68
17. Chapter 17	74
18. Chapter 18	76
19. Chapter 19	79
20. Chapter 20	82
21. Chapter 21	85
22. Chapter 22	90
23. Chapter 23	95
24. Chapter 24	97
25. Chapter 25	106
26. Chapter 26	110
27. Chapter 27	119
28. Chapter 28	126
29. Chapter 29	135
30. Chapter 30	139
31. Chapter 31	144
32. Chapter 32	154
33. Chapter 33	160
34. Chapter 34	164
35. Chapter 35	169
36. Chapter 36	174

| About Author | 176 |
| Also By | 177 |

This book is dedicated to Dr. Lynn Greenwood, Assistant Professor of Criminal Justice, who let me use her artistic talent for the book cover.

Introduction

They say that your first love never dies. You can put out the flames, but not the fire. — Bonnie Tyler

Chapter 1

Mary Ann McCommas Green stretches in her bed. This is the first day in a long time she didn't wake up to an alarm. She smiles broadly and yawns. Today is the beginning of a new life, she thinks. Well, it almost is. Today is the first day of retirement. Well, technically, I'm on vacation for a month, and then retirement begins. After thirty years in the Arizona Public School System, I am out of there. She sits on the side of her bed and looks around the bedroom of her apartment. Soon, I'll be out of here and in my home for a change.

Mary Ann surveys the bedroom furniture, reaches to her nightstand, and picks up her checklist. Then, glancing over at the items she has already checked off, she looks around the room again. Her grandmother's dressing table, brought from Ireland, has already been picked up to be refinished. Along with it was Mary Ann's mother's dining room table and chairs and a few other sentimental items she decided to take with her.

Today's item on the checklist is to go to her new home in Peoria and measure all the rooms. After that, Mary Ann will have to go furniture shopping since she decided to get new everything for her home. That includes new linens, dishes, and so on, but first furniture. Mary Ann has been researching online and already has a good idea of what she wants and the color scheme for the house.

With a growing excitement for a new future, Mary Ann hops in the shower and dresses quickly. Then, grabbing her laser measuring tape, legal pad, and purse, she heads out the door for the twenty-minute drive to the new house. As she drives, Mary Ann thinks about her new home. She bought a small two-bedroom, two-bath house in a retirement community. The house is five years old, and the previous owner is now in a nursing facility. Fifty homes surround a well-maintained park and pool in a small development. She doesn't have a family to visit, so the small house is perfect. Well, there is Dillon, her son, but she hasn't seen or spoken to him in years. Just the thought of Dillon brings tears to her eyes because Mary Ann does not know why Dillon stopped talking to her.

She shakes her head to clear her thoughts. No, I refuse to let the past interfere with today, Mary Ann decides. I have a lot to do before moving out of the apartment, so I can't dwell on unpleasant thoughts. Arriving at the house, she parks in the driveway and gets out of the SUV. Mary Ann walks to the front of the house and pulls up the For Sale sign in the yard.

"Hi! You must be the new owner." Mary Ann turns to her right and sees a gray-haired man in khakis and a polo shirt walking in her direction. "Here, let me get that for you," the man says, reaching for the sign.

"Hi, yourself. Thanks for the help," Mary Ann says, releasing her hold on the sign. "Yes, I'm the new owner, Mary Ann Green."

"I'm Sam Forsyth, your next-door neighbor." Sam leans the sign against the garage and turns to Mary Ann. "They'll pick up the sign in a day or two. It's great to meet you. It'll be nice to have someone closer to my age as a neighbor. When will you be moving in?"

"I'm not exactly sure yet. I need to clean and buy furniture first," Mary Ann laughs.

"Is there anything I can do to help?"

"No, but thanks for the offer."

"Okay," Sam replies. "Just ring the doorbell if you change your mind." He gives Mary Ann a massive grin before turning to return to his house.

Mary Ann watches him walk away. Nice-looking, personable guy, she thinks, with an impressive body. She turns and walks to the front door. After unlocking the door and stepping inside, Mary Ann stands for a few seconds looking over her new house, a feeling of excitement growing in her heart.

I better get moving and get these rooms measured. It doesn't take long to measure and draw diagrams of each room. Next, Mary Ann studies the measurements of the furniture she is bringing with her and places it in the diagrams. Now, I can furnish the rooms with the new stuff. After a couple of hours of work, Mary Ann is satisfied and heads to a nearby furniture store she found online with a vast selection.

It takes four hours, but Mary Ann finds everything she needs and wants at the store. Several items will need to be ordered in her colors and patterns, but they can deliver all the furniture in two weeks.

By now, Mary Ann realizes she not only skipped breakfast but lunch as well. So she stops on her way home to eat and then to the food store to buy enough food for the next two weeks. Mary Ann also stops to purchase boxes, tape, and packing materials. It is after 5:00 pm, by the time Mary Ann arrives back at the apartment. The day's excitement has made her tired, so after unloading her SUV and putting her food away, she sits down to watch television.

Chapter 2

The following two weeks pass by swiftly. First, Mary Ann had the carpet cleaned at the new house and had the entire house repainted. Then she thoroughly cleaned the house. Sam, her new neighbor, came by twice to say hello and offer to help. Once, he invited Mary Ann over for coffee, but she refused, saying she was in a rhythm and hated to stop.

On Wednesday of the second week, Mary Ann receives the call she has been waiting for. All the new furniture will be delivered on Friday, and she is ready. The furniture she sent out to be refinished is already in place.

Mary Ann is at the house early on Friday morning. The furniture arrives at 9:00 am, and the employees unload and unwrap the furniture. Sam brings over coffee. He and Mary Ann stand outside watching the progress. She glances up and down the street and smiles as she sees curtains moving in neighboring houses. I think everyone appears to be taking an interest in my life. I hope that's not a bad thing.

Then, Mary Ann sees a car across the street backing out of the driveway. This is the first time she has seen any activity at the house. As the car pulls forward on the road, a man looks over at Mary Ann. Wow! He's gorgeous, she thinks, looking directly at him.

"That's William," Sam says in a gruff voice. "William, not Bill. He's not friendly."

"I haven't met him yet," Mary Ann states, noticing the change in Sam's voice.

"Few people have. He keeps to himself, although several of the women in the neighborhood have tried very hard to get his attention."

"Oh, okay," is the only thing Mary Ann can think to say.

"He's nothing like me. I'm friendly to everyone, especially the ladies."

Mary Ann looks into Sam's eyes and sees a glint of something dark that makes her uneasy. "Thanks for the coffee, Sam. It looks like they are ready to move items in, and I need to tell them where to place them. I'll talk to you later." She notices Sam hesitates before heading back to his house. If he thinks I was going to invite him in to help, he is mistaken; she thinks as she walks into the house.

It has been a long day by the time Mary Ann returns to the apartment. Tired but eager to move into the house, she reviews her checklist. Tomorrow, she shops for linens, dishes, and pots and pans. After a quick shower, Mary Ann climbs into bed and falls asleep.

The third week of moving into the new house is hectic for Mary Ann. First, she launders all the new linens and takes them and the new dishes, pots, and pans to the new house. Then she finishes packing up the apartment. The movers will come on Friday and move all the boxes to her new place. Mary Ann got lucky with the apartment furniture. The landlord agreed to keep all the furniture and rent the apartment furnished to the next tenant.

Now that everything is moved into the new house, Mary Ann spends the last week cleaning the apartment, changing her address, and finally turning in her keys. As she leaves the apartment for the last time, she sighs. This apartment has been home for the past five years. Although it was convenient for her work, Mary Ann never felt at home, so leaving is easy. Besides, a whole new life full of experiences awaits her in Peoria. There will be new people to meet, including that gorgeous man across the street she has seen only once since they delivered the furniture.

Chapter 3

Waking up in her new house, free of the apartment, and fully retired, Mary Ann steps out into her backyard with her first cup of coffee. She feels relaxed and at peace. The backyard fence affords her the luxury of remaining in her gown without fear of being seen or judged. So she sits down on the patio, sipping her coffee and enjoying the view of the mountains.

Mary Ann ponders the mountains in the distance. I go to the mountains on June 15th every year. The day and location where Mark proposed to me forty years ago. A tightness in her chest threatens to choke the air out of her. After all these years, the memory of Mark and the happy times we had still affects me. I guess it always will, Mary Ann decides. But I don't want to think about sad things today. I just want to enjoy my new home and status.

When the coffee cup is empty, Mary Ann looks down at her wrist for the time. She smiles because she put her wristwatch away in her jewelry armoire last night. Beginning today, there are no schedules, deadlines, or appointments that she needs to be mindful of. Mary Ann walks into her kitchen and looks at the clock on the microwave. It is 6:45 am, so she gets her robe and goes outside to retrieve her newspaper.

As she bends over to grab the paper, the garage door across the street opens, and the gorgeous neighbor backs out. Mary Ann stands as the garage door closes while Mr. Gorgeous backs onto the street. She notices he rolls down his window as he passes and observes Mary Ann watching him. Finally, he nods, rolls the window up, and drives off.

Gorgeous but pompous, she decides, turning back toward the house across the street.

"Yes, he's a handsome guy, but not friendly at all," a female voice from next door says.

Mary Ann turns to see a woman about her age picking up her newspaper. "Hi, I'm Mary Ann."

"I know," says the neighbor. "I'm Greta. Sam has made sure everyone is aware of your name. Well, everyone but William. They don't speak. Welcome to the neighborhood."

"It's nice to meet you, Greta, and thanks. I look forward to getting to know everyone."

"You'll get to meet them at the end of the week."

"End of the week?"

"Oh, I guess you didn't get the neighborhood newsletter. Friday is our first Friday potluck. The neighborhood association buys some type of meat. Usually chicken or BBQ and everyone else brings a vegetable or dessert. We meet at the community center across the park."

"That sounds like fun," Mary Ann states.

"It is. We play games, and there's a lot of talking. Well, mostly gossiping, I guess. You'll soon figure out who to avoid," Greta says with a hearty laugh.

"What time does it start?"

"We gather about 6:00 pm and eat first. I hope you can come."

"I'll be there, and thanks for letting me know."

Greta nods and starts walking toward her house. She stops and turns to Mary Ann. "Watch out for Sam. He's a player and a businessperson. You'll see." Before Mary Ann can say anything, Greta quickly walks into her house and closes the door.

That was an interesting comment about Sam, Mary Ann contemplates. I could tell he was a player, but the business person comment is odd. She walks to the house, gets another coffee, and takes it and the paper to the patio.

Later, after breakfast and dressing, Mary Ann gets out her cookbooks to plan on her dish for the potluck. She's been to enough potlucks that she is aware of the typical dishes older women take to such events. Mary Ann wants to take something other than a macaroni, gelatin salad, or sheet cake.

She decides on a dessert that includes whipped cream, vanilla and chocolate pudding with a shortbread crust. It is one of her favorites that her mother made. Mark loved it, too. Why has Mark popped back into her mind again? I haven't thought about him in a while. Maybe it's because our wedding anniversary is coming up soon. I doubt he remembers. After all, he left right after our third one.

Mary Ann lists everything she will need for the dessert and several other items before heading for the food store. When she returns and everything is put away, Mary Ann changes into her two-piece swimsuit. She studies herself in the mirror. Not back for a sixty-year-old woman with one child. I tried to keep myself in shape. I guess I did a reasonably good job. She grabs her coverup and heads to the pool next to the community center.

Several people are at the pool when Mary Ann arrives. Some wave, and some ignore her. She goes over to a vacant chaise, removes her coverup, and lays it and her towel down. She walks around the pool to the shallow area and selects a spot, and steps in. The water feels heavenly. When she looks up, Mary Ann is face to face with Mr. Gorgeous.

"Oh, I'm sorry," she says, looking into his dark brown eyes. "The water felt so good. I wasn't paying attention."

The dark brown eyes study her for a few moments. Then Mr. Gorgeous says, "be a little more careful next time," and he swims away from her.

"You don't have to be such as ass about it," Mary Ann says aloud without thinking.

Mr. Gorgeous turns around and sees Mary Ann turn a bright shade of pink. "An ass?"

Unaware, everyone around the pool is watching her; Mary Ann replies, "yes, an ass. I said I was sorry."

"Sorry for almost bumping into me, or sorry for calling me an ass?" Mr. Gorgeous asks, tilting his head to one side and smirking.

"For almost bumping into you. I'm definitely not sorry for calling you an ass. Now, not only are you rude, but you're smirking at me."

"Mary Ann, I was not rude, but I am smirking. To be nicer, please excuse me while I get out of the pool."

"So you're sarcastic as well. You must get a lot of women with your personality," Mary Ann retorts before turning and wading in the opposite direction, not allowing Mr. Gorgeous time to comment.

She feels Mr. Gorgeous watching her wade away from him and studies her for a few seconds. Then he swims to the side of the pool. Leaning against the poolside, Mr. Gorgeous watches Mary Ann climb out of the pool and walk to her chaise. Once she is lying down, he climbs out of the pool and walks over to her side, unaware everyone is staring at him.

Looking down at her closed eyes, Mr. Gorgeous clears his throat, causing Mary Ann to swiftly open her eyes.

"What is it now? Am I in your reserved chaise? How do you know my name?" Mary Ann says heatedly, looking into the dark brown eyes.

Without asking, Mr. Gorgeous sits down on her chaise, forcing Mary Ann to move her legs to the side. "You just moved in across the street from me. I know your name because Sam makes it his business to know everything about everybody. That means you know my name is William. You are not in my chaise. If you were, I wouldn't ask you to move because you're beautiful." William, AKA Mr. Gorgeous, stands and leaves.

Stunned by his comment, Mary Ann watches William walk away from her. His stance is relaxed and confident. His shoulders are broad, and his waist is tapered at the beginning of his trunks. Beneath his trunks are muscular, tanned legs.

As if William knows Mary Ann is watching him, he turns, winks, and smiles with a huge smile at her. This time, she doesn't blush. Instead, she stares, appreciating the view but wondering about the mysterious neighbor across the street. He walks to his chaise, picks up his towel, and leaves the pool area.

Three women rush over to Mary Ann when William is out of view. One woman says William has never spoken to her. Another comments William is soooo hot. Finally, the third says why did he talk to you? Mary Ann stares at the three, excuses herself, and leaves the women wondering what Mary Ann has they don't.

Mary Ann returns home just as William pulls into his driveway from the opposite direction. She looks his way, but he ignores her. "Ass," she says aloud to herself.

"There you are. I rang your doorbell, and you didn't answer," Sam yells from his front porch. He walks toward Mary Ann. "I assume you went to the pool."

Mary Ann rolls her eyes before looking at him. "Good guess, Sam. Did you need something?"

"I was going to ask if you knew about the potluck Friday and if you would like to go with me."

"Greta told me about the potluck this morning. Thanks for the invitation, but I think I'll go alone," Mary Ann answers secretly, hoping William will be there.

"Oh, okay. Please have dinner with me on Tuesday of next week?"

"That's an entire week away. I'll have to check my calendar and get back to you," Mary Ann replies.

"Yeah, I have a pretty full schedule with all the single ladies in the area," Sam says, winking at Mary Ann.

"I bet you do," Mary Ann answers sarcastically. Thankfully, Sam doesn't catch the sarcasm, but William does and laughs aloud. Mary Ann turns to see William watering his plants next to the curb. "I'll let you know about next week, Sam." She gives William a dirty look and walks toward her house, leaving Sam alone in her yard.

"What are you looking at?" Mary Ann hears Sam yell at William.

"According to you, a man with a busy dating schedule. Haven't the women around here figured out yet that you're just using them for sex?" William answers.

"Go to hell," Sam yells at William and stomps back to his house while William laughs and laughs.

Well, that was interesting, Mary Ann thinks. They don't like each other. That's plain to see. I may go out to dinner with Sam once, but as far as sex with him, that's a big no. Now, if it were William, I might have to consider it.

Chapter 4

Mary Ann walks to the community center on Friday night with her dessert. She estimates around seventy-five people are there. Greta sees Mary Ann and rushes to meet her. She takes her around the group, introducing Mary Ann to the people Greta knows, and they both meet newcomers along the way.

Of course, Sam is there and gives both Mary Ann and Greta a kiss on the cheek when he walks up to them. Mary Ann notices a slight coolness in the way Greta greets Sam, although she is polite with him. Sam doesn't linger but makes his way to a group of what Mary Ann assumes are single women.

Hoping to see William, Mary Ann wanders around the groups after dinner and chats with each briefly. But William is nowhere to be found. So, once she has socialized all she cares to, Mary Ann takes her empty dessert dish and walks home. At least it was a hit, she decides. So many requested the dessert again next time.

It surprises her to see several vehicles parked at William's house. Well, no wonder he wasn't there, Mary Ann thinks as she goes inside her house. The vehicles prove that he's not a total hermit, just an ass.

Chapter 5

Mary Ann spends every day at the pool for the next month hoping to see William. She hasn't seen him leave his house either, so she assumes he must have gone on a trip. She has avoided having dinner with Sam, which gives her a feeling of relief for some unknown reason.

During the month, Mary Ann observed the street she lives on by sitting in a chair by the front window reading. In one house next door to William lives a very elderly woman who does not leave her home. Instead, people stop by to visit her and appear to bring supplies whenever the elderly lady needs them. The house appeared unlived in on the other side of William. When Mary Ann commented on the house to Sam, he stated that the couple that owns it only live there during winter months.

Others from the street walk by and wave if Mary Ann is outside. A few people stop to talk, but otherwise, everyone appears to keep to themselves. Many mornings, Mary Ann and Greta shared coffee. Greta also retired from the Arizona Public School System, where she had taught for thirty years and retired five years ago. She taught in a school district in northern Arizona, so she and Mary Ann never had an occasion to meet.

Sam is a different story as far as not being very social. Sam is gone for one or two days several times during the month. When he is home, three or four cars visit his house daily. Five to six vehicles visit the next day when he returns home from being away.

Mary Ann wants to ask Greta about the strange things she sees at Sam's house, but she decides against it. Mary Ann doesn't want to get the reputation of being a busybody.

On the last day of the month, it surprises Mary Ann to see William's car pull into his driveway. But, of course, she couldn't see anything because he parked in the garage and immediately closed the door. So at least he's okay, she decides.

Then a new idea comes to mind. I should get an animal for the company since I own my home now. I could get a cat. They require little maintenance if I want to travel. Mary Ann gets up, drives to the nearest no-kill shelter, and falls in love with an orange tabby. She makes all the arrangements to adopt it, but doesn't take it directly home. Instead, Mary Ann leaves the kitten there while she goes to the pet store next door. She spends a small fortune on everything the salesperson said she will need for a kitten. Only then does Mary Ann return to the shelter for the kitten, and she and Lucy, the kitten, go home.

After arriving home and getting Lucy settled, Mary Ann realizes that two items she purchased from the pet store have to be assembled. So she gets in her car and drives to the nearest hardware store for a set of screwdrivers.

Standing in the aisle, looking at the various selections of screwdrivers, Mary Ann feels lost. She turns to leave the aisle and find a salesperson when William walks up beside her.

"Mary Ann, you look confused," Willam says with a half-grin.

"Well, if it isn't William, the ass. Have you come to rescue me?" Mary Ann replies with a smile.

"Yes, ma'am. I followed you here on purpose, knowing you didn't know a thing about screwdrivers. So, what have you gotten yourself into?"

Mary Ann blushes and looks into William's dark brown eyes with curiosity, trying to read him, but she fails miserably. "I adopted a cat and bought two things that must be assembled. First, I need a set of screwdrivers. I did not know there were so many kinds."

William laughs, and his voice changes to a deeper, softer voice that arouses Mary Ann's interest. "Lucky for you, I came along. Did you bring the screw with you?"

"No, but I took a picture of the instructions," she answers, pulling her phone from her purse. She finds the picture and hands William the phone. "Will that work?"

"Yes, it works. This is a basic non-metric Phillips head screw." William reaches for the shelf past Mary Ann. She gets a whiff of a woodsy blend of cologne and body wash as he does. William pulls his hand back, containing a package of assorted Phillips head screwdrivers. "This package should work." William hands Mary Ann the package, which she inspects for several seconds.

"Thank you."

"Mary Ann, have you ever owned a home?" She shakes her head, looking up at him. He takes the package from her and places it back on the shelf. "Come with me." William puts his palm on the small of her back. The touch of his hand sends sparks throughout Mary Ann's body as he guides her to another aisle.

"Now, the consummate homeowner needs an assortment of tools. Do you own any tools?" William asks with his signature smirk.

Mary Ann tries to act offended and fails. "I have a hammer, a level, and laser measuring tape."

William looks into her eyes as she looks up at him. "I feel you are lacking many things," he whispers, looking away quickly. "You need an assortment of tools and a toolbox," he says as he points to the shelves. "Do you mind if I pick one out for you?"

"Please do. I'm at a total loss."

William looks over the tool sets as Mary Ann watches him. He is wearing a short-sleeved t-shirt that shows off the muscles in his arms, across his back, and across his chest. She sees a sprinkling of hair peeking out of his collar. Mary Ann looks down and sees a pair of flip-flops on two perfectly shaped feet.

"Do you like anything that appeals to you?" William asks, turning his head to look at her.

Mary Ann blushes when she realizes he is talking about the tool sets. "No, you decide," she stammers as William gives her his biggest smile. She feels he can read her mind. "I'm sorry to take up so much of your time. I know you came here for a reason."

"I did, but what I need won't fit into my car. So I'll have to come back another time."

"If it would fit into my SUV, I would be happy to take it to your house. It's the least I can do after helping me."

"I think this one will do. That's unnecessary. I'll borrow a pickup and come back tomorrow."

Mary Ann peers at the handsome man in front of her, not wanting to end her time with him. "It's not a problem, really."

"Okay, then. Let's go get it, and we'll check out," William says. He places his hand on her back and guiding her to another department.

William purchases an electric saw while Mary Ann buys her toolset. He pushes the basket to Mary Ann's SUV and loads the saw.

"Follow me home, and I'll open the garage. You can back in. I'll unload the saw." Mary Ann nods and gets into her car. She watches William's backside in those tight jeans as he walks to his car. Mary Ann feels a tingling sensation run through her body.

After the saw is unloaded, Mary Ann gets back in her SUV to drive across the street to her house. William taps on her window, and she rolls it down.

"Mary Ann, can I give you some advice?" She nods. "Stay away from Sam. He's bad news."

"In what way?'

"In every way. Please, just take my advice."

"Okay, William. Thanks for everything." He backs away, and she pulls across the street into her garage and closes the door.

Mary Ann thinks that was an odd encounter, walking into the house with her new tools. Lucy comes running to meet her, so Mary Ann sets the tools down and picks up Lucy. "Hey, Lucy. It's dinnertime. Are you hungry?" Lucy meows loudly, so Mary Ann feeds her and then feeds herself.

After
dinner, Mary Ann tells Lucy about running into William at the hardware store.
The kitten purrs and listens for a few moments before falling asleep in Mary
Ann's arms.

Chapter 6

The following day, William backs out of his driveway as Mary Ann bends over to pick up her newspaper. He uncharacteristically stops at the end of her driveway and rolls his window down.

"How's your new roommate this morning?" he asks.

"She's waiting for breakfast and her scratching post."

"Do you need any help?"

Mary Ann stares at William like he's grown another head. "No, I think I can manage now that I have the right tools. I appreciate all your help yesterday. You should come over sometime and meet Lucy. She's just a baby."

"I might just take you up on your offer. Must run. Bye, Mary Ann." William drives off.

As she returns to her house, Greta comes running out her door.

"Did I just see William stop and talk to you?"

Mary Ann laughs. "Good morning to you, too. Yes, you did. Come in and have coffee. I'll tell you about it, and you can meet my new roommate, Lucy. Oh, wait. Are you allergic to cats?"

"No, I had one until she passed away last year."

"Good. Come on in, then."

Over coffee and holding the kitten, Mary Ann explains seeing William at the hardware store yesterday and how helpful he was. Greta is shocked and tells Mary Ann that William doesn't talk to anyone and keeps to himself.

Changing the subject, Mary Ann brings up Sam. "Greta, what is it about Sam? William warned me to stay away from him."

Greta studies Mary Ann for a few seconds before answering. "I don't know firsthand, but I can tell you what I've heard. I've been told he is the drug supplier for the neighborhood. He sells painkillers and just about anything else anyone could want. I told you he was a player. I've heard he's been known to spread an STD around, too. That caused enormous problems."

"Oh my. No wonder you and William warned me. He makes me very uncomfortable when I'm around him."

"Good. Keep it that way. Lucy is a doll. I'm not ready to get another cat, but if you ever want to travel, I'll be happy to take care of her." Then Greta finishes her coffee and heads home.

Mary Ann showers and dresses as Lucy sleeps on the unmade bed. Rather than disturbing Lucy, Mary Ann goes to work assembling the scratching post and multi-level cat tree. She finishes at lunchtime when there's a knock on her door.

Opening the door, Mary Ann is shocked to find William. "William, what a pleasant surprise. Please come in."

"I just wanted to check on you and your extensive construction project," he says, walking into the house.

"Great timing on your part. I just finished." Then Lucy walks in and heads straight for William, yawning as she walks.

William bends over and picks Lucy up. "Well, aren't you a big girl? She's cute, Mary Ann. I can see why you picked her."

"She picked me. I was about to make a sandwich. Will you join me?"

Mary Ann is blessed with a huge smile. "Thank you. I would like that if it's not too much trouble."

"No trouble at all. Come into the kitchen. I hope you like BLTs."

"I love BLTs. Can I help?"

"No, you're helping plenty by holding Lucy. She's so small that I'm afraid I'll step on her. Please sit down."

William sits at the breakfast table with Lucy stretched out on his lap. He is rubbing her stomach, and the kitten purrs loudly.

Mary Ann makes the sandwiches while she and William discuss the weather. When she's finished, Mary Ann sits the plates on the table along with glasses of water.

William sets Lucy down and heads to the bathroom to wash his hands. When he returns and sits down, he asks, "how do you enjoy living here so far?"

"I love it," Mary Ann replies. "I didn't know what to expect buying in a senior living community. I guess I expected a lot of older people, but I've been pleasantly surprised. There are many activities if you want to take part. How long have you lived here, and do you like it?"

"I've lived here for two years. I like that it's quiet and people leave you alone," William answers and begins eating. "I like my privacy," he says, signaling to Mary Ann not to ask questions.

The two people eat in silence for several minutes. Then William says, "Mary Ann, I'm not seeking a relationship."

Mary Ann almost chokes on her food. "Oh, well, I wasn't even thinking about that. I just hoped we could be friends. I don't want a relationship either." She looks into William's eyes and sees uncertainty.

William stares at her. "We all have secrets that are best left secrets." He plops the last bite of his sandwich in his mouth and pushes his chair back from the table. "I better go. Thanks for the sandwich and for introducing Lucy." He gives Mary Ann a small smile and stands. "I rarely cook, so I can appreciate a homemade BLT."

Mary Ann looks under the table and sees Lucy asleep, curled at her feet, before pushing her chair back. "Thanks for the company," she says, standing.

"I'll see myself out," William states as he walks out of the kitchen.

Mary Ann remains standing in place until she hears the front door close. Lucy wakes and meows. "Lucy, that was very odd," Mary Ann says, reaching for the kitten.

Chapter 7

Two weeks go by before Mary Ann sees William again. She is in her kitchen cleaning when he knocks on her door.

"William, what a surprise. Please come in. Can I get you anything, like something cold to drink?"

"Hi, Mary Ann. No, thanks for the offer. Am I interrupting anything?"

"Yes, I was mopping the kitchen floor. Want to help?" she asks with a laugh.

"No, I'll pass. I was wondering if you would like to have dinner with me one night?"

"I would like that because I tire of eating my cooking."

"Are you free tomorrow night?"

"Yes, I am."

"Great. Why don't we meet at that new Italian place on Avenue E? Will 7:00 pm work for you?"

"Yeah, sure. 7:00 is good."

William smiles and says, "good. I'll see you there. Have fun mopping the kitchen." He turns and strides out the door.

Lucy wanders in from the bedroom. "Lucy, I don't understand him. He asks me to dinner and then I have to meet him there. That man is a weird. Maybe it's him I should avoid as well as Sam."

The next evening, Mary Ann pulls into the restaurant's parking lot. Since it didn't sound like a date invitation, she chose a short-sleeved sundress and sandals. Mary Ann also brought a light sweater in case the restaurant was chilly. She gets out of her car and sees William's car several rows over without him. She shakes her head and walks to the restaurant, confused.

William is waiting for Mary Ann inside and stands as she enters. "I got here a few minutes early because there's always a wait to be seated," he says. She nods and looks around the restaurant.

William's name is called, and he follows the maitre d' to the table with Mary Ann behind him. He sits down and opens the menu as Mary Ann seats herself.

The server brings water, bread, and butter to the table and asks what the couple would like to drink.

William speaks first. "I'll have a glass of your house red wine."

The server looks at Mary Ann, confused. "I'll just have water, thank you," Mary Ann states. The server nods and leaves after flashing Mary Ann a look of sympathy. She picks up the menu and reads over it, trying not to look at William.

When the server returns with William's wine, he asks if they are ready to order.

"I'll have the Fettuccine Alfredo and salad with house dressing, William states.

The server writes the order and looks at Mary Ann. She looks up at the server with tears forming in her eyes. "I'm not hungry. William, this was a mistake. Enjoy your dinner without me." Mary Ann stands and hurries out of the restaurant to her car.

Once inside, she starts the car and puts it into gear. As she is backing out of the parking space, Mary Ann sees William come out of the restaurant, heading her way. She ignores him and drives home as fast as she can.

Once inside the house, Mary Ann bursts into tears after picking Lucy up. "I have never been so insulted in my life," she cries. "That was a massive mistake on my part." Carrying Lucy into the bedroom, Mary Ann changes into shorts and a t-shirt and then gets a frozen dinner. She shoves it into the microwave and sits down, waiting for it to be ready.

After dinner, Mary Ann goes out on the patio and sits down, looking at the mountains in the distance. Mark would have never treated me that way, she thinks. But, on the contrary, he was always the most considerate man I ever knew.

Suddenly tears flow down Mary Ann's cheeks as her still wounded heart yearns for the man she married forty-three years ago and hasn't seen in forty years. The man that left her without an explanation. Mark just stopped coming home.

Mark was two years older than Mary Ann and one of the high school's "bad" boys. He rode a motorcycle and hung out with a rough crowd. She had heard about the group but had never actually seen them. Until Mary Ann's sixteenth birthday. The day fell on Friday, June 1, and she and two friends had gone to a drive-in movie. Mary Ann had gone to the snack bar to get popcorn and a drink when she heard the motorcycles pull up. Two of the motorcycles halted in front of her, blocking her way.

One guy got off his motorcycle and looked directly at her. He was the most handsome boy Mary Ann had ever seen. He had black hair that reached below his ears. His eyes were a dark shade of green, and his nose was slightly crooked, probably from a fight, Mary Ann assumed. His lips were full, and his chin was strong.

Her eyes traveled down the length of his body, slowly beginning at the neckline of his black t-shirt. She saw a sprinkling of black chest hair peeking out. The black jacket covered the t-shirt except for the muscles of his chest that the material of the t-shirt couldn't hide. The black jeans fit snugly around his waist and the big silver buckle he wore caught her eye. His legs tapered down to black boots that fit his calves just as snugly as the jeans around his thighs.

Mary Ann's eyes traveled back up his body, and she saw those green eyes staring at her. Suddenly she felt hot from a heat inside rather than outside her body. The boy approached her, looking deeply into her eyes. Mary Ann wanted to look away, but she couldn't.

He stopped in front of her so close Mary Ann could feel his breath on her face. The boy reached up and touched her cheek with his fingertips.

"You are the most beautiful girl I have ever seen," he said. "Some day I will marry you and we'll make beautiful babies together."

Still mesmerized by the green eyes, Mary Ann nodded slowly, holding her breath. Then the spell was broken by another boy yelling, "Mark!" Mark turned and looked at the other boy, saying, "Just a minute, Ross."

Then he turned back to Mary Ann. "I'm serious," he said. "You will be my wife one day." Then, Mark gently kissed her as if to seal his promise to her before turning and walking away.

A knock at her front door interrupts Mary Ann's memories. Knowing it is probably William, she takes her time answering.

When she opens the door, William says, "what the hell was that all about?" walking into the house.

Mary Ann slams the door and turns to him with her hands on her hips. "I have never been so humiliated in all my life."

"What are you talking about?" William yells.

"Did your mother not teach you any manners?" Mary Ann yells back.

"It wasn't a date, Mary Ann!"

"I know it wasn't, but you could still have treated me respectfully."

William looks at her, confused, and then shakes his head. "Can we sit down?" he asks. Mary Ann points to the sofa. William sits down, and Mary Ann continues to stand, looking down at him full of righteous anger.

"Mary Ann, you're right. I'm very sorry. It's just that I have been nowhere with a woman in a long time. I have manners. My mom taught me well. But I'm used to eating out with men, and they don't expect manners."

"You should have thought of that before you asked me for dinner," Mary Ann says sharply.

"Can I make it up to you? I promise to use manners this time."

"I'll think about it. Now, please go." William stands and sees the hurt and anger in Mary Ann's eyes. He walks past her and out the door.

"Odd man," she tells Lucy, who has emerged from the bedroom, yawning and stretching. "I'm going back outside, but I must feed you first, little girl."

Once back on the patio, Mary Ann's thoughts pick up where she left off. She had watched the boy walk away, admiring how the back of his jeans fit his behind so perfectly. Mary Ann quickly returned to her friend's car.

"Where's your drink and popcorn?" her friend, Natalie, asked.

"I got cornered by the motorcycle group and forgot all about it."

Dee, Mary Ann's other friend, asks, "did you see Mark?"

Not wanting to reveal too much, Mary Ann said, "which one is Mark?"

Natalie let out a loud sigh. "Have you been living under a rock? He's the handsome one with black hair and the most amazing green eyes you can imagine."

"Ross isn't bad looking either," Dee stated.

"I saw Mark, and he spoke to me," Mary Ann told them. "He said he would marry me one day." Natalie and Dee laughed.

"He probably says that to all the girls so he can get into their panties," Dee said. "He is hot. Too bad we won't see him anymore?"

Mary Ann's head turned in Dee's direction. "What do you mean?"

"He and the rest of the group just graduated. That is a shame, too. None of the guys in our or the senior class are that good-looking. I used to see Mark in the hallway occasionally," Natalie answered.

"I was in Algebra with Mark and I stared at him the whole class. That's why I had so much homework," Dee laughed. "Let's watch the rest of the movie, and then we'll get something to drink."

Mary Ann didn't see the movie. Instead, she sat in the backseat and remembered the way Mark's green eyes peered into hers, and how she felt an unfamiliar stirring in her lower abdomen.

The following morning, Mary Ann awoke to her dad's booming voice. "Mary Ann, get down here now."

She jumped out of bed and put her robe on before running down the stairs. Something serious must have happened, she thought. Dad never yelled like that. Mary Ann was out of breath by the time she reached the kitchen.

"What is it, dad?"

Her dad and mom stood around the dining room table. Both had serious expressions on their faces. Mary Ann's dad pointed to the middle of the dining room table, where a long-stemmed red rose lay on a bed of green florist wrapping paper.

"What is this?" he said, pointing at the rose.

"A rose," Mary Ann answered, bursting into laughter.

"I'm serious, young lady. It's not for your mother and me, so that leaves you," her dad said.

"I don't know, dad. Where did it come from?" Mary Ann asked.

"It was lying on top of the newspaper this morning."

Mary Ann's mother smiled and said, "maybe it's a late birthday gift, or Mary Ann could have a secret admirer."

"Or it is a mistake," Mary Ann said. "I can check with the florist to find out if you like."

"No, let it go. I'll get a vase for it," Mary Ann's mother stated, winking at Mary Ann.

Mary Ann opens her eyes and realizes the darkness has set in while she was lost in her memories. So she goes inside and gets ready for bed. Lucy is already snuggled up on the bed, so Mary Ann carefully climbs in beside her, so Lucy doesn't wake.

Chapter 8

Sleep doesn't come for Mary Ann, even though her eyes are heavy, and she can't stop yawning. Giving in to her memories, she begins by remembering a red rose appeared every Saturday morning until school started. No one ever admitted the rose was from them, but Mary Ann believed the roses came from Mark.

The first day of her junior year began with the excitement of a new school year and the promises it brought. Mary Ann put her things into her assigned locker before she headed to her first class. She planned not to visit the locker until lunch, so she took all the books she would need for her morning classes.

Mary Ann went to put her books and notebook into her locker before joining her friends for lunch. Everyone had to supply their lock with two keys to their lockers. They kept one key in the principal's office if someone lost or forgot theirs. So it shocked Mary Ann when she opened her locker to find a red rose lying on top of her stuff. She looked around and didn't see anyone suspicious. She closed the locker, smiled, and went to lunch. Mary Ann left the rose in the locker all week as a reminder that someone, hopefully, Mark, cared about her. She hid the rose from her friends because she didn't want to answer questions.

That Friday night, Mary Ann, Dee, and Natalie went to a movie at a downtown theater. During intermission, Mary Ann stepped outside feeling a little dizzy because the theater was hot. Standing on the sidewalk alone, it surprised Mary Ann when a hand touched her shoulder. She immediately knew who it was by the heat she felt all the way to her toes.

"Mark," she whispered.

"Hi, Kitten," he whispered in her ear. His hot breath tickled. "Can you talk for a few minutes?"

Mary Ann turned to face him and looked into those green eyes that pulled her in. "Yes," she whispered breathlessly.

"Let's step over here out of the way." Mark took her arm and guided her next to the building, away from passersby.

"Mark, thank you for the roses. They were beautiful," Mary Ann said in a low voice.

"Beautiful roses for a beautiful girl. I hoped you would know they were from me. I didn't want you to think I forgot about you."

Mary Ann stepped closer to Mark, so her chest almost touched his. She looked at him and said, "I could never forget about you."

Mark stared into her eyes and asks, "Kitten, are you allowed to date because I want to take you out?"

"Yes, I can, but I don't think my dad would allow me on a motorcycle."

"Let me worry about that. Would you have dinner with me tomorrow night?"

"I would love to have dinner with you." Mary Ann watched as Mark's green eyes sparkled in the neon lights above their heads.

"Great. I'll pick you up at 7:00. What's your curfew?"

"It is 11:00. Oh, you'll have to meet my mom and dad. House rules."

"Okay, not a problem. I'll be on my best behavior. After all, I'll ask their permission to marry you one day, so I need to make a good impression."

Mary Ann couldn't help herself. She reached up and touched his cheek. Mark grabbed her hand and leaned into her touch. Then he lightly kissed her lips.

"You better get back inside," he said, removing her hand from his cheek and guided her toward the theater door.

Back in reality, Mary Ann looks over at the clock and sees it is 1:00 am. She turns over, closes her eyes, and falls asleep dreaming of those green eyes.

Chapter 9

Mary Ann turns off the alarm to sleep a little longer, but Lucy wants to play. Laughing, Mary Ann plays with the kitten before they both get out of bed. Unfortunately, Lucy demands to be fed before Mary Ann can even go to the bathroom. After feeding Lucy, Mary Ann brews coffee and heads to the bathroom for a shower. Mary Ann has learned that there is no such thing as privacy with a kitten in the house, so she leaves the door wide open.

Showered and dressed, Mary Ann makes her way to the kitchen and makes toast. She is still angry with William and gets her newspaper after she's sure he has left. Holding Lucy, Mary Ann eats her toast and has her first cup of coffee. When Lucy heads to the bedroom, Mary Ann pours another cup of coffee and goes to the patio. She stands gazing at the mountains.

Mary Ann ponders why the memories of Mark are returning now. Is it because of William and the forgotten feelings he stirs? Or is it because she yearns for Mark in her heart, although she does not know where he is? All Mary Ann knows is that Mark always refused to sign the divorce papers, so technically, she and Mark are still married. Married? What a joke that is. He left her. Why? She thought she was a good wife, but maybe not good enough. Did he find another woman? I do not know, and I always refused to ask Dillon about his father.

She shakes her head and estimates William has left by now. Mary Ann gets her newspaper and refills her cup before returning to the patio. She opens the newspaper but doesn't read. Oh, Mary Ann had male friends, lovers, and even a couple of relationships that could have turned serious if she had let them. Those two men fell in love with her, but she couldn't love them back. Plus, she never fully trusted any man after Mark. Mary Ann didn't want to be hurt again because the pain of Mark leaving never left her. Besides, she couldn't have married anyone, anyway, because she is still a married woman.

Mary Ann thinks back to her and Mark's first date. He drove up in an older car and came to the door to get her. Her dad answered the door and invited Mark in. Mark introduced himself to Mary Ann's mom and dad. They talked for a few minutes while Mary Ann tried to eavesdrop on the stairs. She couldn't hear, though, and her heart was pounding with anxiety.

Finally, Mary Ann's mom called her name, signaling it was time for her to appear. Mary Ann picked a sleeveless blue cotton sundress with a light sweater. She knew the blue dress would bring out the blue in her eyes and make her blonde hair appear brighter. Mary Ann wore ballerina flats since she did not know what the date would be.

Once at the bottom of the stairs, Mary Ann took a deep breath and rounded the corner into the living room. She looked at Mark, who gave her a 1,000-watt smile, and Mary Ann knew she had picked the right dress. Mark reached for her hand while Mary Ann's dad reminded the young couple of the curfew time.

FORTY YEARS TOO LATE?

At last, Mark and Mary Ann could escape. He held her hand all the way to the car and opened the door for her. Then, putting his hand on her back, he guided her into the car and closed the door. Mark got in and drove off slowly, much to the appreciation of Mary Ann's dad, who Mary Ann saw watching from the window.

"I bet you're glad that's over with," Mary Ann said with a smile, looking over at Mark.

"It wasn't so bad. Your parents are very nice."

"I'm sure you got the third degree. This is my first date."

"Really? As beautiful as you are, I would have thought guys would beat down the door to get to you."

"You're sweet, but this is my first date. I never wanted to go out with anyone before," Mary Ann said shyly, looking down at her hands.

Mark smiled broadly. "Well, we're out of sight of your house. Why don't you slide over and sit next to me?" Mary Ann did, and Mark put his arm around her. She blushed at the touch. Mark noticed and said, "you better get used to it. I'll be doing it as long as I'm physically able." He squeezed her shoulder.

The couple rode in silence the short distance to the pizza parlor. Mary Ann slid to the other side of the car, but Mark stopped her. "We are getting out on this side." He opened the door and reached for Mary Ann's hand. He guided her out the door. Mark closed the door and put his hand on the small of her back, guiding Mary Ann into the restaurant.

Once inside and seated in a booth, Mark asked what she v like to drink. Mary Ann replied a soda. Then they disc˙ pizza choices. She preferred beef, and Mark liked r they decided on one-half beef and one-half per cheese. There was no discussion about the was only thin crust pizza back then.

Mark left for a few minutes to place their order. When he returned, Mark was carrying their drinks. Mark slid into the booth beside Mary Ann and put his arm around her shoulders. He pulled her close enough to smell the lavender scent of her soap and shampoo.

Mary Ann deeply inhaled Mark's combination scent of wood and musk. His protective arm stirred feelings deep inside her, just as every touch had so far. Mark asked Mary Ann about school, her hobbies, and extracurricular activities. It seemed he wanted to know everything about her. He talked about his job as a motorcycle mechanic and how much he enjoyed working with his hands.

Mary Ann asked about the motorcycle group and Mark's "bad" boy image. He explained the group was just a bunch of guys that like to hang out and ride motorcycles. As far as his image, he did not know where that came from.

Once the pizza was ready and Mark's name was called, he went to get the pizza, plates, and napkins. The couple ate and continued to talk. They are only children and grew up in the town. Mark explained that he still lived with his parents but was saving for an apartment. His parents live in another part of town, which Mary Ann knew isn't the best part of town.

While they ate, several people they knew came in and stopped by to say hello to the couple. Mark and Mary Ann introduced each other to anyone the other didn't know.

Once they finished eating, Mark checked the time and told Mary Ann he didn't want her to be late on their first date. However, they still had a couple of hours, and Mark suggested going for a drive.

Mary Ann assumed he was headed for Lover's Leap, a popular ⁀t for making out. But Mark surprised her and drove to a hill overlooked the town. He could tell Mary Ann was nervous, so

Mark removed his arm from her shoulders and placed both hands on the steering wheel. Then he sensed her relax.

"Kitten, I never want you to feel uncomfortable with me. I will always treat you with respect."

"Thank you. I just. Well, I never," Mary Ann stammered and couldn't seem to get the words out.

"I know, Kitten. I won't rush you. We'll know when it's time, and I want it to be special for you, for both of us."

"Have you?"

"Yes, but it was just sex. Guys need that sort of thing. I was serious about marrying you. I don't want to have sex with you because I want to make love to you."

Mary Ann considered his words for several minutes. Then Mark took her hand and squeezed it tightly.

"I'm serious, and I hope you know that. I won't ever cheat on you. The minute I saw you, I fell in love with you. You are the only woman for me."

They spent the rest of the night talking and getting to know each other. Then, Mark took Mary Ann home fifteen minutes early, hoping to make a good impression on her parents. Mark asked her out again for the following week, and Mary Ann accepted.

Mary Ann reaches for her coffee and is surprised to find it is cold. I guess I walked down memory lane longer than I thought. Mark told me that night I was the only woman for him. I wonder if that changed after we got married. I just wish I knew what I did wrong for him to leave me.

Well, that's enough thinking for today. I have things to do, so I better get started. So, Mary Ann gets up and goes into the house, leaving the memories on the patio for the time being.

Chapter 10

Determined to keep any thoughts of Mark at bay, Mary Ann works in her yard until almost dark for three straight days. She and Greta have coffee on those days, and Sam walks over to ask Mary Ann out to dinner again. She tells him she has plans for the night when he asks her out.

On the fourth day, she is potting some new plants she bought to give a little color to her front yard. Mary Ann is bent over with her back to the street when she hears, "Hey!" Without turning around, she knows it's William.

"Hey," Mary Ann responds.

"I take it you're still mad at me," William says, walking over to her.

Mary Ann straightens up and looks directly at him. "Maybe. No. I don't know."

"Okay." William gives her his big smile. "My offer for a do-over for dinner is still open. I've been practicing my manners with the help of a friend." He squats down beside the decorative pot Mary Ann is working on.

"Practicing with your blow-up doll?"

William falls over laughing.

"William, you better get up. I'm sure you've given the neighbors enough of a show."

He looks into Mary Ann's eyes and sees her eyes crinkle with a smile. "You're probably right." William stands and takes a step closer to her. "I'm sure some are already on the phone gossiping. Well, what about dinner tomorrow night?"

"I'm leaving on a trip the day after tomorrow, so I'll be packing tomorrow night."

"Okay, what about tonight, then?"

Mary Ann thinks for a few moments and then says, "okay, but not that same restaurant. I don't think I could deal with the server's pity again."

William shakes his head. "Fine. I'll be here at 7:00." He turns and walks back to his house while Mary Ann admires the view of his muscular back and calves.

Promptly at 7:00, William knocks on Mary Ann's door. When she opens the door, she sees him dressed in black jeans and a light gray button-down shirt. Momentarily surprised at seeing William dressed in something other than a t-shirt or polo, Mary Ann looks away.

"Maybe I should change," Mary Ann says, looking down at her capris.

"No, you look great. Are you ready to go?"

Mary Ann nods and reaches for her purse, wondering what surprises this night will have in store. Since William picks her up, she has no escape if things turn sour.

William steps aside as Mary Ann steps over the threshold and locks the door. He takes her elbow and guides her to his car, where he opens the door for her. Once she is inside, he closes the door and gets into the car himself.

"Do you like Chinese? I know a great little place in another part of town," William states.

"I love Chinese and I haven't found an excellent restaurant yet, so I'm excited to try it." Mary Ann sees curtains move in several houses as William guides the car down the street. She smiles, knowing the shock the neighbors are experiencing.

On the ride to the restaurant, William asks Mary Ann about her new plants. She explains she doesn't have a green thumb but will try anything once. William tells her he loves plants and has several in his backyard that he babies throughout the year.

When they reach the restaurant, William is a perfect gentleman. He opens the car door, guides Mary Ann into the restaurant, and lets her go first to be seated. Once seated and given the menu, they discuss drinks and food. Mary Ann orders first, and then William provides the server with his order.

After the server leaves, Mary Ann smiles at William and says, "so far, so good."

He laughs. "The evening is still young, though. You said you were going on a trip. Would you like me to take care of Lucy while you're away?"

"Thanks, but Lucy is staying with Greta while I'm gone."

"Greta?"

"The lady next door to me."

"Oh, I didn't know that was her name," William replies.

Mary Ann rolls her eyes at him. "Do you know anyone on our street?"

"Just you and Sam, who I wish I didn't know."

"Greta told me about Sam. I've been avoiding him as much as possible."

William reaches over and touches Mary Ann's hand. "Good. He's trouble in so many ways. May I ask where you're going?"

Mary Ann talks about her trip to Arkansas that she tries to make yearly while they eat.

"I assume you're going alone," William says, looking into Mary Ann's eyes.

"If that's your way of finding out my marital status, yes. I'm going alone. I'm married, but we've been separated for years."

"Really? That's unusual."

"I'll say. My husband would never sign the divorce papers. So I gave up sending them to him a long time ago. I haven't seen him in the whole time we've been separated."

"What happened, if you don't mind me asking?"

Mary Ann looks down at the table. "I don't know. He just stopped coming home one day. He was a great father to our son and saw him every weekend."

"So, you have a son?"

"Look, William. I don't want to talk about all that tonight. Now, reveal a secret or two about yourself. It's only fair, you know."

"Okay. My wife died many years ago. I have two sons and a daughter who live nearby. We try to get together once or twice a month."

Mary Ann reaches across the table, laying her hand on William's. "I'm sorry about your wife."

"It's fine. It was a long time ago," he says wistfully. "I guess I never got over it. That's why I'm not looking for a relationship. I don't want to be hurt again."

"I can certainly understand that." Mary Ann hesitates and says, "why don't we just be friends?"

"I like that idea very much."

Mary Ann feels a warmth run through her body. He agreed to be friends, she thinks. Maybe, we could be friends with benefits.

"Why are you blushing?" William asks.

"Sorry, I just got a little warm. Are you warm?"

William moves his hand and softly touches Mary Ann's cheek. "Yes, it is a little warm in here."

The topic over dinner returns to Mary Ann's travel experiences, which fascinate William. He tells her he has traveled little in his life but would like to start.

Soon dinner is over, and William takes Mary Ann home. When he walks her to the door, she invites him inside. Lucy comes meowing from the bedroom, demanding attention. William picks her up and holds her while Mary Ann makes coffee. Lucy entertains the couple while they drink their coffee but soon tires and heads back to the bedroom.

William stands and says, "I better go." Mary Ann follows him to the door. "Mary Ann, I enjoyed tonight. I hope I passed inspection and you'll have dinner with me again."

"You passed. Why don't I cook for you when I get back? I'm a pretty good cook."

William takes a couple of steps forward and stops when he is close enough for Mary Ann to feel the heat from his body. "I would enjoy a home-cooked meal."

William leans over, placing a soft kiss on her lips. He looks at Mary Ann as if asking permission to kiss her again. She responds by leaning into him and touching her top lip with the tip of her tongue. William's hand slides around her waist, pulling Mary Ann into him, and his lips meet hers again. There's a hunger in his kiss that she responds to. Suddenly, William stops and takes a step back.

"Mary Ann, I'm sorry."

"I'm not," she says, reaching up to touch his face. "I think I would like you to do it again."

"Another time, perhaps." William turns and walks out the door.

Mary Ann closes the door behind him and leans against it. That man is confusing, she decides and heads to the bedroom to join Lucy, who is fast asleep in the middle of the bed.

Chapter 11

The kitten wakes Mary Ann at 1:00 am, wanting to play. It's just as well, Mary Ann thinks. Mark was invading my dreams, anyway. It takes forty-five minutes for the kitten to wind down, jump off the bed, and go to God knows where. Mary Ann is wide awake but lies down, hoping to go back to sleep, but it doesn't work. I guess William's kiss brought back memories of Mark; she determines and brings a few happy moments to mind.

Mary Ann woke to her dad's voice the following morning after her first date with Mark. She slept little because she relived the date over and over.

"Mary Ann, get up and come down for breakfast." Mary Ann scrambled to brush her teeth and rushed down the stairs. The table was set, and a red rose lay on her plate.

"I think it's safe to assume all the roses came from Mark," her dad said.

"Yes, dad. When school started, they were in my locker before lunch period on Mondays. They still are." Mary Ann watched the looks pass between her mom and dad as her mom places breakfast on the table.

"Mary Ann, just how long have you known Mark?" her mom asked.

"I met him the night of my birthday, but I wasn't around him at all until he asked me out the other night."

Another look passed between her parents. Then her mom said, "I just don't want you to fall for the first guy that asks you out. We don't want you to know hurt, is all."

"Mary Ann," her dad began. "Boys that age have too many hormones in their bodies." Mary Ann dropped her fork. This is the first time her dad has ever said anything like that to her. "I don't want you to get into a situation you can't control. You can always call your mom or me, and we will come to get you wherever you are."

"Dad, Mark was and is a perfect gentleman."

"Well, last night he was," Mary Ann's father said. "Boys like Mark have been around, if you get my drift. They can change quickly."

"Look, honey," Mary Ann's mom starts, "We just want you to be careful. Now, on a different subject, you, Dee, and Natalie spend a great deal of time on the phone. Now that Mark's in the picture, he will probably call too. So your dad and I think it's time for you to have your own phone."

"That's right, Mary Ann," her dad agreed. "I'll call the phone company Monday morning and get your very own phone installed in your room. Then your mom can have her phone back, since I don't seem to get any calls." All three laughed.

"Thanks, mom and dad. Can I use the car this afternoon?"

"Sure," her mom answers. "I'll finish my shopping after breakfast, and then you can have it all afternoon."

The phone rang, and Mary Ann ran to answer it. "Hey, mom, dad, would it be okay if Mark comes over late this afternoon?"

"Of course, but Mary Ann, ask him to come for dinner. We'll cook out on the grill," her dad answered. He heard his daughter talk into the phone and then hang up.

Mary Ann walked back into the kitchen and kissed her dad's forehead. "Thanks, dad. I told him to come about 6:00."

After breakfast, Mary Ann grabbed the telephone book and rushed to her room. Lying across her bed, she looked up the address of the motorcycle shop Mark worked at. She needed to see Mark more than once a week, so what better way to do that than get a job after school near where he worked?

Mary Ann turned over and considered her parents' concern. I know they are afraid I'll get hurt, but I have to try. I will also be able to see if Mark is serious about marrying me someday.

After lunch, Mary Ann drove by the motorcycle shop, which was closed for the weekend. She drove around several times and looked at the different businesses in the area. Next, Mary Ann bought a newspaper and looked over the jobs listed in the paper. She found a law office that was seeking a file clerk to work three evenings a week from 4:00 to 7:00. Memorizing the address, Mary Ann drove around until she found the building. It was two blocks from the motorcycle shop.

Mary Ann planned to borrow the car Monday afternoon and apply for the job. She had spent countless hours working in the principal's office, so that should count for experience, Mary Ann determined. Plus, she might get to see Mark after he got off work. With a plan in mind, Mary Ann rushed home to shower and dress to prepare for Mark coming to dinner.

Mark arrived promptly at 6:00. Mary Ann took him into the backyard, where her dad already had the grill going.

"Hi, Mark! I hope you like burgers," Mary Ann's dad said, offering his hand to Mark.

"I do, Mr. McCommas. The breeze off the mountains has cooled things off today," Mark replied.

"Hi, Mark. I'm so glad you could join us," Mary Ann's mother said. "I made lemonade. Would you like a glass?"

"Yes, ma'am. Thank you for the invitation," Mark said with a big smile as he took the offered glass.

"Why don't you two sit in the shade while we work," Mary Ann's dad said, pointing toward four lawn chairs.

Mark nodded and placed his hand on Mary Ann's back. He guided her to the chairs. Once seated, the young couple whispered about their day. Mark worked until noon at the shop. He told Mary Ann he had difficulty concentrating on his job because he was thinking of her. Then, Mary Ann told him about her idea for a job near his work. Mark got excited about the prospect and told her he would see that she got home safely every night if she got the job.

After the dinner of burgers, Mr. and Mrs. McCommas talked with Mark and Mary Ann until dark. When they went inside, Mary Ann retrieved a blanket so she and Mark could lie in the backyard. The young couple didn't lie close together but held hands. Mark pointed out different constellations to Mary Ann, impressing her with his knowledge.

At 10:00, Mark told Mary Ann he should go home. He helped her fold the blanket and carried it into the house. Mark told Mr. and Mrs. McCommas good night after thanking them again for dinner. Mary Ann walked Mark out to the car, hoping he will kiss her goodnight. Instead, he kissed the back of Mary Ann's hand and brushed a stray lock of hair behind her ear. His fingertips slid across her cheek, making Mary Ann tingle all over.

"Kitten, I hate to leave you, but I'll call you."

"Mark, mom and dad are getting me my own phone. I'll give you the number as soon as I know what it is."

"And let me know about the job. Have you told your parents?"

"Not yet. I don't know how they will react."

"Like I said, I'll make sure you get home every night. So be sure to tell them that, okay?" Mary Ann nodded. "Good night, my precious kitten." Mark got in the car and drove off, watching Mary Ann in the rearview mirror.

Finally, Mary Ann is getting drowsy, and Lucy has returned to bed, snuggled against Mary Ann's back, so they both drift off to sleep.

Mary Ann hits the snooze button several times before climbing out of bed. She wants to stay longer but needs to prepare for her trip tomorrow. While she showers, Mary Ann thinks about her trip. She's flying to Tulsa and rented a convertible to drive to Eureka Springs. Her cousin, Audrey, is meeting her at the cabin for three days of shopping and relaxation.

After her shower, Mary Ann checks the Eureka Springs weather and then packs. She will take Lucy over to Greta's before she leaves in the morning if she doesn't pack her in the suitcase.

Mary Ann goes to bed early since she slept little last night. As she climbs into bed, her phone pings with a message. Mary Ann sees the message and is shocked to see it is from William.

"Hurry back. I miss you already," the message says.

Well, that came out of nowhere, she thinks. Mary Ann replies with a smiling emoji, turns over, and goes to sleep.

Chapter 12

When Mary Ann returns and goes to Greta's to get Lucy, she senses Greta has something important to tell her. "Greta, was Lucy okay while I was gone?"

"Lucy was a perfect angel. It's William and Sam I need to tell you about," Greta says.

"Oh, what happened?"

"They almost got into a fistfight in Sam's front yard. They were yelling at each other. Everyone was at their windows watching."

"What was the fight about?" Mary Ann asks.

"You. It was about you."

"Me?"

"Yes, Sam told William to stay away from you. Sam said he would tell you some big secret about William. Well, not only you, but everyone in the neighborhood," Greta says.

"Oh, my gosh!"

"William threatened to kill Sam if he told anyone, especially you. And William told Sam to keep away from you, too. He said you had already been warned about Sam, his business, and misdeeds. Then, at last, security showed up and broke up the argument."

"Wow! That sounds serious."

"It was a little scary. Do you have any opinion on what secret William may have?"

"No, William talks very little about himself. He said his wife died a long time ago, and that he has three kids. That's all he's said about anything personal."

Greta watches Mary Ann for several seconds. "You're not falling for the guy, are you? I mean, he is good-looking and all."

Mary Ann laughs. "I don't think dinner and coffee qualify as falling for the guy. We have both agreed we aren't looking for a relationship."

"Well, just be careful," Greta warns. "I don't want you hurt."

Mary Ann is back from her trip three days before William knocks on her door. "Hi, Willam," she says, opening the door. "Come in, and I'll make coffee." He walks inside, and Mary Ann closes the door. When she turns around, William pulls her to him and kisses her.

Surprised, she doesn't respond at first, so he leans back and looks at her. Mary Ann reaches for his neck and pulls his lips back to hers. When she feels his tongue touching her lips, she opens them and invites him into her mouth. The kiss turns deeper. William tastes of coffee and William to her. Mary Ann runs her fingers through his hair, savoring the kiss.

William's lips move to her earlobe and down her neck to her clavicle. The heat he causes inside Mary Ann makes her pant. Having a man kiss her and hold her in his arms feels so good.

"William," she whispers. "Did you miss me?"

His lips move back up to her earlobe. He licks around the outside of her ear. "I missed you so much," he says, his breath tickling her ear. "Did you miss me?"

"Yes. Yes, I did."

Willams leans back and looks at Mary Ann. She sees his dark eyes scorching her with desire. "I'm glad to hear that." He releases her. "I think you said something about coffee. I think now would be a good time." His voice is deep and husky.

Mary Ann nods and heads to the kitchen, with William following close behind. Lucy greets him with a loud meow. He picks up the kitten and talks to it while Mary Ann brews the coffee.

"Did you have a pleasant trip?" William asks.

"I did. My cousin met me at the cabin, and we shopped and shopped."

"I'm glad to hear that. It was quiet around here while you were gone."

Mary Ann glances at William out of the corner of her eye. "Well, it is a quiet neighborhood, but then, that's why we moved here, isn't it?"

They talk about Mary Ann's trip while they have their coffee. William gives no indication about the argument with Sam. When they finish, William invites Mary Ann over to his house the next night for dinner. He tells her he will cook out on the grill so they can sit outside and appreciate the cooler evenings.

Mary Ann is on her way out the door to William's house when she receives a message from him.

"The side gate is unlocked, so come on back."

"Well," she says aloud. "So much for seeing the inside of his house. He is weird." Mary Ann does as she's told and walks to the side of the house and opens the gate. She is stunned to see a beautiful garden with so many types of plants in full bloom. Mary Ann steps inside the yard, looks to her right, and sees William in front of a grill.

"Hi, Mary Ann. Come on in," William says with a big smile.

"William, it is beautiful back here. It's like an oasis in the middle of a desert."

"Thanks. Now you know what I do in my spare time. I built all the planters you see. Can I get you a glass of wine?"

"That would be so refreshing," Mary Ann replies, walking over to him. Instead of getting the wine, William pulls her into his arms and kisses her passionately. Mary Ann returns the kiss, driven by her need for a man's touch. She breaks off the kiss and says, "wow! What a hello."

William smiles with a dark yearning in his eyes. "I wonder what a good night will be like. Maybe there won't be a good night. But, on the other hand, it may be a good morning."

Mary Ann caresses his cheek. "I guess we will have to wait and see." She leans into his body as close as she can. William responds by planting little bites and kisses down Mary Ann's neck, across the top of her tank top, and up the other side of her neck.

"I think you forgot to wear a bra tonight," William whispers in her ear.

"Should I go back and put one on?" Mary Ann pants.

"No, I think you should go topless." Willams leans away from her and reaches for the hem of her top. "No one can see us." He pulls her top off and then steps back to admire the view of Mary Ann's breasts. "That's much better," he smiles.

"I think it's your turn," Mary Ann says, reaching for William's t-shirt. He lets her pull it over his head and then takes her into his arms again.

"Mary Ann, it's been so long since I've touched a woman's body. You feel incredible."

"Then touch all you want to," Mary Ann replies.

William reaches over and turns off the grill. He takes Mary Ann's hand and leads her into his house and bedroom. William finishes undressing Mary Ann and undresses himself. The couple has sex, but it is almost mechanically, like following instructions on a building project.

"That wasn't so good, I know," William says, holding Mary Ann in his arm. "I am out of practice."

"It will get better," Mary Ann assures him, but in her mind, she thinks, I wonder if it will.

Later that night, lying in her bed, Mary Ann thinks about what happened at William's house. After a nice dinner, the couple had sex again, and then she went home. Willam asked her to spend the night, but she refused. I'm not ready for that, Mary Ann told him.

Chapter 13

The next three months fly by swiftly. Mary Ann and William become a popular item in the neighborhood. They spend almost every day together and many nights.

At the end of the three months, William presents Mary Ann with a gift over coffee after spending another night together.

"William, you shouldn't have," Mary Ann says as he hands her a small gift-wrapped box.

"It saw it, and it made me think of you."

Mary Ann opens the gift and finds a beautiful gold necklace with a cat pendant. The cat's eyes are green emeralds that resemble Lucy's. "William, it's beautiful. Will you put it on?"

William nods and kisses Mary Ann's neck as he fastens the necklace. Then he says, "I know we both agree not to get into a relationship, but what we have seems more than friends with benefits."

"I agree," Mary Ann says. "Maybe we could say we are going together as we did back in the day."

"I'm good with that," laughs William.

"Now, I need to go. I'm leaving this afternoon and have lots to do."

"Okay, but stay in touch with me, so I know you're fine," William says, kissing her cheek as she rises to go home.

Once home, Mary Ann sits down to show Lucy the necklace. Then she does laundry and packs. Mary Ann is only going to the mountains for a couple of days, but the weather is unpredictable, so she over packs. She understands she will have to relive her memories if she plans to have any sort of relationship with William. Mary Ann has to do it. It happens every time she becomes interested in a man.

Mary Ann hasn't thought about Mark for several months, but the drive to the mountains causes the memories to surface. Mary Ann got the job at the attorney's office, so she got to see Mark on Tuesday, Wednesday, and Thursday evenings. True to his word, Mark always made sure Mary Ann got home.

Friday night was their date night. Mark told Mary Ann early on that he made little money, so dinner out was a once weekly occurrence. They usually spent Saturdays at Mary Ann's house or Mark's house. On Sunday, they went for drives. Mary Ann didn't care where they went or what they did. She just wanted to be with Mark. Mary Ann knew she was falling in love with Mark after their first month together. She had talked to her aunt about her feelings and the unfamiliar sensations that ran through her body when Mark touched her.

Mark was always the perfect gentleman and never got fresh. Mark had asked her permission when he really kissed her for the first time. That kiss sent Mary Ann over the edge. She knew it wouldn't be long before she would want to be Mark's in every way.

Mary Ann pulls into the parking lot of one of her favorite places. She gets out and climbs to the outlook Mark first brought her to.

It was where he proposed. Although she makes a pilgrimage here on that proposal day each year, Mary Ann felt a need to come now. I guess it's the memories that have stirred in my heart and mind that have brought me here; she considers.

Mary Ann sits down on the big rock overlooking the mountains. She lets the memories wash over her. Mary Ann and Mark were happy together and in love. Every week, a red rose showed up in her locker at school. Then, when the school year ended, they showed up on Saturday morning with the newspaper.

Mary Ann's parents liked Mark a lot, and his parents liked her. Life was grand. The week before Mary Ann's birthday, Mark asked her what she wanted for a birthday gift. Mary Ann thought about it while the couple lay on the car's hood looking at the stars.

"Mark, I've given it a lot of thought," she said, sitting up and facing him. "I've tried to fight these feelings inside me, but I'm tired of fighting them. I want to be yours in every possible way. That's what I want for my birthday."

He sat up, took her hand, and looked into her eyes, where he saw her love for him. "Kitten, are you sure? I would love that very much, but I want you to be sure."

"I am sure, Mark. It's time. Please, will you give me that gift?"

"Yes, Kitten," Mark said reverently, caressing her cheek. "It will be my honor to be the first man to make love to you." He slid off the car and pulled her to him. He took her into his arms, so she wouldn't see the tears of happiness in his eyes, but she felt them on her shoulder.

Mark picked Mary Ann up at 5:00 pm on her seventeenth birthday. He drove to his apartment, which he got a couple of months earlier. Mark asked her to stay in the car for a few minutes until he came out to get her. Mary Ann was confused, but did as he asked. She had already been to his apartment several times.

After several minutes, Mark came to the car and got her. When he opened the apartment door, the room smelled of lavender. Grasping Mary Ann's hand, Mark guided her to his bedroom. Lit candles were everywhere, and red rose petals covered the open bed.

"Oh, Mark, this is beautiful," Mary Ann exclaimed with tears in her eyes.

"Are you sure you want to do this?" he asked.

"I need to be yours," Mary Ann whispered.

Mark welcomed her into his embrace and kissed her over and over. Each time, the kiss became more passionate—the fire of desire consuming them. Mark began slowly undressing Mary Ann, giving her time to change her mind. But she didn't. She watched every movement he made with a smile.

Once she was undressed, Mark took a step back and looked at Mary Ann's body. Then, he told her to lie down on the bed. Mary Ann did so and watched as Mark undressed. His naked body sent shivers down her spine, and fire ran through her blood vessels.

"This is your last chance to change your mind," Mark said as he lay down next to her.

"Don't stop. Please, don't stop."

Mark began kissing her. He kissed every part of her body, working his way from her forehead to her toes. It was as if he was worshiping her body, Mary Ann thought. Soon it was time.

"Kitten, this will hurt, but only for a few seconds," Mark told her. She nodded, and he entered her. Mark was right. But the pain stopped, and then the pleasure began. Mark started slowly and then increased his speed as he felt Mary Ann's body relax and enjoy the sensation.

Mark made it last as long as he physically could. When it was over, he gently laid down on top of Mary Ann, covering her with his body. Mark became alarmed when he looked at her and saw she was crying.

"Kitten, are you okay? Did I hurt you too much?"

"These are tears of joy," Mary Ann answered. "Mark, I love you so much," she whispered.

"I love you too, Kitten. I love you more than I ever thought possible." Mark rolled over and took her into his arms, lying there for a long time. Mark said, "I have something for you." He got off the bed and went into the kitchen.

Mark was carrying a cupcake with a single lit candle when he returned. "Happy Birthday, my love."

Mary Ann blew out the candle. "I don't want to eat it now," she said shyly, looking down.

"Can I get you something to drink?" Mark asked, sitting the cupcake beside the bed.

Mary Ann reaches up, puts her hands around his neck, and turns him to her. "I want more," she whispered in Mark's ear.

"Well, my love. It is your birthday, and I am more than happy to help you celebrate," he says, giving her his 1,000-watt smile.

Mary Ann realizes she has tears running down her cheeks. The memory of Mark making love to her for the first time sends her into a tailspin. She sobs her heart out. The crying continues until Mary Ann is gasping for breath.

Mark was the best lover she had ever had. He was patient and kind and always put her pleasure before his own. Oh, how she missed his lovemaking even after all these years. Mary Ann knew, if she had the chance, she would move heaven and earth to be in his arms and bed again. But that will never happen, she decides. So, I will have to be stuck with mechanical William for the time being.

Mary Ann looks at the mountains again. She wipes her eyes and nose before heading back to the SUV to drive to the hotel.

Chapter 14

Mary Ann booked a balcony room so she could sit outside and enjoy the cooler temperatures. On the way to the hotel, she stopped to buy two bottles of her favorite red wine. Now, having had dinner, Mary Ann sits on the balcony with a glass of wine. She looks at the wine, which is almost blood red. The memories flood her mind again.

Mark and Mary Ann couldn't get enough of each other after their first night of making love. Each time became more intense, more passionate. It was like they were trying to absorb each other.

Then, two months later, Mary Ann showed up unexpectedly at Mark's apartment. She was crying.

"Kitten, come in," Mark said when he opened the door to find her standing there. "Why are you crying?" He reached for her and held her tight. "Let's sit down, and you tell me what's wrong." Mark led her to his sofa, sat down, and pulled her into his lap.

Mary Ann took a few seconds to get the words out between sobs. "Mark, I think I'm pregnant. I'm pretty sure I am." She looked at Mark, not knowing what to expect. She had prepared herself for anger.

"Really, Kitten? You think you're pregnant?" Mary Ann nodded. Then confusion overtook her tears. Mark was smiling. He noticed the confusion on her face. "What's wrong?"

"I, I thought you would be mad," stammered Mary Ann.

"Mad? Oh no, Kitten. I'm thrilled. Mark lifted her and sat her down on the sofa beside him. He stood up and started dancing around the apartment. Mary Ann watched Mark and decided he had lost his mind.

"Kitten, I guess I should apologize for not taking precautions, but I thought you were on the pill."

"Mark, what the hell is wrong with you? This changes everything."

He knelt in front of her and took her hands in his. "Kitten, do you love me?" he asked solemnly.

"Mark, I love you more than anything in the world."

"Do you want this baby?" Mary Ann nodded. "Great. We can work this out. We can be a family."

Mary Ann shakes her head. She looks down and realizes the wine bottle is half empty. She pours another glass and leans her head back against the back of the chair. By now, the sun has set over the mountains.

Things changed for Mary Ann and Mark. Mark took an afternoon off and accompanied Mary Ann to a nearby clinic that confirmed she was pregnant. Next, together they told both sets of parents. Mary Ann wasn't showing yet, but she quit school and went to work at the law firm full time.

Mark brought Mary Ann to the overlook on his motorcycle one week later. He had packed a picnic lunch, and after eating, they lay on the blanket looking at the clouds floating by. Suddenly, Mark stood and pulled Mary Ann to her feet. He pointed for her to sit on the big rock. Wondering what Mark was up to, Mary Ann did as instructed.

He pulled a gorgeous small diamond ring from his pocket and proposed to her. Mary Ann said yes, tears rolling down her cheeks.'

"Mark, this ring is beautiful," Mary Ann said as he slid it on her finger.

"It was my grandmother's. She gave it and the wedding ring to me before she died. She told me to give it to my wife."

"I will wear it forever and cherish our love." She stood, and they hugged, holding each other with the intention of it being forever.

Two days later, Mr. and Mrs. Mark Green emerged from the courthouse smiling. Two crying mothers and two unhappy fathers followed them. Mary Ann moved into the apartment. It was convenient since it was within walking distance of the law firm and the motorcycle shop. The couple walked to work together every morning, ate their lunch together in the park, and then walked home together after work.

Mary Ann took her GRE test and passed, which resulted in a sizeable raise from the law firm. Mark worked overtime at the motorcycle shop to earn extra money for the baby. Mark could also sell motorcycles which paid a nice commission. He always took a break each afternoon to walk Mary Ann home and then returned to the shop.

Mary Ann and Mark realized they also needed a break from each other. So on Friday nights, Mark rode motorcycles with his friends while Mary Ann hung out with Dee and Natalie. Mary Ann grew bigger and bigger with Baby Green.

At the beginning of Mary Ann's eighth month, she answered a knock on the apartment door and was surprised to find her parents. They visited often, but usually called first.

"Hi," Mark said, walking in from the bedroom. "This is a pleasant surprise."

"Mark, Mary Ann, we want to talk to you," Mary Ann's dad began.

"Okay, let's sit down," Mark said.

"We've been talking," Mary Ann's dad said, pointing at Mary Ann's mother. "This apartment is small, and you'll need more room for the baby. So we want you to move in with us for a while."

Mary Ann's mother spoke up then. "You can have Mary Ann's old bedroom, and we'll turn my sewing room into a nursery. Then, after the baby comes, I can keep the baby while you both work."

Mary Ann was shocked and looked over at Mark, holding her hand. Ever the gentleman, Mark said, "that's a very generous offer, and we thank you. Can we think about it a few days and let you know?"

"Sure," Mary Ann's dad said. "We would love to have you. Mark, you are our son now, and family should be together."

Mary Ann's parents stay a little longer. Then they leave the couple to talk and decide.

Mary Ann says aloud, "I've finished that bottle of wine. I guess I should go to bed and get a fresh start in the morning."

Chapter 15

The alarm goes off, and Mary Ann awakes with a headache. I shouldn't have drank all that wine; she determines climbing out of bed to get aspirin. After a shower and breakfast, Mary Ann feels ready to tackle the memories. She drives back out to the outlook and sits on the rock.

Gazing at the mountains, Mary Ann hears Mark's voice in her head. "That was a very generous offer your parents made."

"Yes, and a surprise, too," Mary Ann said the following night when the couple sat down to discuss it. "They had a good point because we will need a babysitter while we work."

"That's true, but I don't want my parents to be jealous of all the time we spend with your parents," Mark said thoughtfully.

"What if we try to spend every Sunday with your parents and maybe one evening during the week?"

Mark thought a few seconds and then said, "that would work. But, Mary Ann, I don't want to live with your parents for free."

"I agree. We can negotiate a payment with them to cover rent and food. I can also buy food instead of mom. We will have to drive to work, though. It's too far to walk."

"That's no problem. We can ride together, and I'll bring you home every afternoon. You shouldn't be walking much longer, anyway." Mark reached over and rubbed her belly. The baby kicked at that moment as if in agreement, causing the couple to laugh. "The baby is getting more and more active."

"Definitely. It seems to always be more active when I'm talking to a client. Sometimes, I have to apologize. But, fortunately, everyone is very understanding," Mary Ann said, putting her hand over Mark's.

Mark used his other hand to caress Mary Ann's cheek. "I'm so lucky to have you. I can't imagine life without you. And I can't wait to meet our baby."

"You're going to be a great dad, Mark. I love you so much," Mary Ann said, leaning over to kiss him. "Let's make love, and maybe we can rock the baby to sleep." Mark helped Mary Ann up, and they went into the bedroom.

The couple moved in with Mary Ann's parents at the start of her ninth month. Mr. and Mrs. McCommas refused to accept any rent payment but agreed to let Mark and Mary Ann buy food every other week. Mary Ann had to take a medical leave from her job, and Mark quit working overtime so he could be home when the baby came.

Mary Ann stops the memories there. Mark was such a wonderful husband. He always told her how beautiful she was, even when she grew to the size of a baby elephant. Mark was very attentive to her every need. She couldn't have designed a more perfect husband. *If only I knew what went wrong,* Mary Ann thinks before continuing.

One January evening, Mary Ann's parents went to dinner with friends. That was the night Baby Green made its appearance. Mark panicked, causing Mary Ann to laugh in between labor pains. Somehow, they made it to the hospital in one piece.

Mark was in the delivery room with her and would leave to call both sets of parents. Unfortunately, he kept forgetting the phone numbers between the delivery room and the pay phone. Finally, the nurse took pity on him and wrote the numbers down.

Soon, it was time. The doctor allowed Mark to watch the entire process and hold the baby as it came out. Mark was crying as much as the baby. The doctor wiped the baby off, and Mark placed their little boy in Mary Ann's arms. Now, all three were crying. Mary Ann remembers Mark kissed her and thanked her.

After the baby was born, Mary Ann worked hard to regain her figure. She went back to work. Mark helped with the baby as much as he could. He enjoyed watching little Dillon grow. Mark was home a lot and was there when Dillon took his first steps. Mary Ann and Mark played with Dillon and read to him at night.

They were so happy, but when Dillon was two, Mark's best friend, Ross, died in a motorcycle accident. Mark was there when it happened. Mark began changing. Mary Ann knew Mark was having a tough time with Ross' death. The two men had been friends since first grade.

Mary Ann tried to get Mark to talk to her, but he refused. So then Mark began drinking more and more heavily and coming home later and later. Mark's attention was on Dillon when he was home, not his wife. Things got worse and worse. Then one night, Mark stopped coming home altogether.

"Ma'am? Ma'am, are you alright?"

Mary Ann looks up to see a young couple standing over her and realizes she is sobbing.

"I'm sorry," Mary Ann says. "I was just remembering something sad."

"We were hiking and heard you," the young woman says.

"Thank you for checking on me. I'm fine," Mary Ann replies.

"Are you sure?" the young man asks. "We would be happy to sit with you for a while."

"No, please continue with your hike. It was very nice of you to stop."

Then the couple starts to leave, but the young woman turns around, bends, and hugs Mary Ann. "Things will get better," she says, leaving Mary Ann to catch up with the young man.

No, things don't get any better in this case, Mary Ann thinks. She wipes her tears away. I don't know what happened. I don't know if Mark found another woman he wanted to be with. I don't know what I did wrong. I know he stopped coming home, and I haven't seen or talked to him since. I caught glimpses of him at Dillon's baseball games and my parents' funerals, but that's all. He never signed the divorce papers, so I could be free to start a new life. It's been forty years and nothing but an emptiness no one but Mark could ever fill. Well, at least he was an excellent dad to Dillon.

Mary Ann stands looking out over the mountains. Then she looks down at her left hand, where she still wears the engagement and wedding rings. She smiles wearily. In seven years, we will have our golden wedding anniversary. So why track down Mark and ask for a divorce now? I will never be free of him. I will never love another man or trust another man the way I did him. But at least he will never be totally free of me, either.

"I'll see you next year on the proposal anniversary, the year after that, and the year after that," Mary Ann tells the mountains and the overlook. "Maybe someday I'll be free of Mark or dead."

Mary Ann returns to her car with a mixture of regret and depression. But, at least now, she has relived the memories and can think about William.

Chapter 16

The following day, Mary Ann barely pulls into her driveway before Greta, holding Lucy, appears at her garage door.

"Greta, hi. Are you okay?"

"Mary Ann, let's go inside. I have news to tell you." Both women walk into the house. "You better make coffee," Greta says.

Mary Ann nods and puts the coffee on to brew. She takes Lucy, holds her, and is welcomed home with loud purrs. "Okay, Greta, sit down and tell me."

Greta sits and says, "the first day you were gone, the police found Sam dead in his car over in the warehouse district of Phoenix. He was shot between the eyes."

"Oh, my gosh!" Mary Ann almost shouts. "Do they know what happened?"

"They are investigating. The police have been here questioning everyone on the street. They came here, but you weren't home. I said you would be back today, so they will probably be here today or tomorrow."

Mary Ann rubs Lucy. "I can't believe someone would kill Sam. I know there were issues, but nothing that serious."

"You should know," Greta pauses, "they asked about the argument between William and Sam. Several neighbors heard William say he would kill Sam."

"Surely, no one thinks William would," Mary Ann states.

"Who knows? William is always so quiet and keeps to himself. Only you know him better than anyone here."

"I don't know him that well. He never talks about himself. It's as if he's full of secrets." Mary Ann gets up to get their coffee.

"Does anyone ever know someone?" Greta asks.

Mary Ann thinks about Mark. "No, I guess we never do."

"How was your trip? Lucy missed you. She's so sweet."

Midafternoon, someone knocks on Mary Ann's door. Expecting to see William, it surprises her to see two men who identify themselves as police detectives. She invites them in and offers coffee, which they decline.

The officers explain they are investigating Sam's death. They ask questions about his activities. Mary Ann tells them Sam always gave her the creeps, although she never knew why. She tells them about Sam leaving for a day or two and the many cars that visited his house the day he returned.

The officers ask about the argument between Sam and William, but Mary Ann explains she was out of town and just heard about it from her neighbor.

"We have been told the argument was about you," one officer states.

"That's what I was told," Mary Ann says.

"Do you have any idea why they would argue over you?"

"All I can tell you is that Sam kept asking me out, and I wouldn't go. I began spending some time with William. I can only assume Sam might have been jealous."

"Mrs. Green, how well do you know Mr. Sanders?"

"Not well."

"Has he ever talked about his past?"

"No, all he's ever said is that his wife died."

The officers leave, telling Mary Ann they may have more questions in the future.

Mary Ann doesn't hear from or see William, but at 6:00 pm, a police car pulls up in front of his house. Two officers go to his door, and William leaves with them.

Mary Ann doesn't hear from William for two days. Then he messages her on the afternoon of the third day.

"Can you come over now? We need to talk."

Curious, Mary Ann immediately walks across the street to William's house. He answers the door as if watching for her.

Expecting William to take her in his arms and kiss her, it shocks Mary Ann when he turns, walks to the living room, and sits on the sofa.

"Okay, William," she says. "You wanted to talk, and I'm here."

"Mary Ann, please sit down. I have something to tell you. I rather you hear it from me than the newspapers or Greta."

"This sounds serious. Does it have to do with Sam's death?"

"In a way, it does." William takes a deep breath and motions for Mary Ann to sit down. She sits in a chair across from him.

"Do you remember I told you my wife died?" Mary Ann nods. "Well, there's more to the story. I married my wife in 1980. We lived in Prescott. I was a firefighter, and she was a stay-at-home mom. We had three kids."

William pauses, looks at Mary Ann briefly, and then looks at the floor. "When our youngest child started school, Katie wanted to get a job. She said she was bored. So she got a job as a secretary at a real estate office. Then one day, Katie disappeared."

Mary Ann stares at William. "What do you mean, she disappeared?"

"She just disappeared in 1991. We were living in Flagstaff. The police found her car about five miles from our house on a dead-end road. Her purse and keys were still in the car."

"Oh, my God. I bet you were crazy with worry," Mary Ann says.

"I was, but that's not the end of the story. In the beginning, the police thought I had done something to her. As a firefighter, I worked twenty-four hours on duty and forty-eight hours off. I was on duty from midnight the day before Katie vanished until midnight the next day. People surrounded me, so there was no way I could have done anything to her."

William pauses and is visibly shaking. "Then the police came up with a theory that I had paid someone to kill Katie. I didn't. We had a happy marriage, I thought. I was happy. Katie seemed happy. Katie always packed the kids' lunches and then took them to school before she went to work. That was her late morning, so she didn't dress for work when she dropped the kids off at school. Several mothers talked to her and said Katie was still in her robe and pajamas."

William takes a breath and puts his head in his hands before continuing. "The youngest boy forgot his lunch, so the school called Katie. She told them she would drop it off on her way to work. Katie dressed for work and then dropped the lunch off. She never made it to work."

"Anyway, everyone in town and the police thought I had caused her disappearance. Police, citizens of the city, and strangers searched and searched for her. They didn't have the technology back then, so it was a ground search. Nothing was ever found. The people in the city made it very hard for my kids and me because they just knew I did something to Katie. After a few months, the kids and I moved in with my parents in Phoenix. My parents helped me raise my kids. Anyway, they found no trace of Katie, so seven years later, I had her declared dead. The kids and I needed to move on with our lives."

William looks over at Mary Ann, who's staring at the floor. "Mary Ann, say something."

She looks up at him slowly. "Why are you telling me this now?"

"Because the police think I may have been involved in Sam's death. I know you know we argued while you were gone. Sam was jealous that we were seeing each other. So he did some research and found out about my past. He thought you would stop seeing me if he told you, and then he could move in on you. I swear to you I did nothing to my wife or Sam. Please believe me, Mary Ann. I need to know you believe me."

"I don't know what to think right now. You should have been honest with me from the beginning. This has blindsided me. I need to go home and think." She rises and walks out of his residence, unsure what to believe.

Back in her house, Mary Ann sits down to digest the information William shared. She vaguely remembers reading about the disappearance. Mary Ann and Dillon were living in Flagstaff at the time.

Mary Ann stayed in her and Mark's tiny house for several months after Mark left, hoping he would return. Then, as a single mother who needed more income, Mary Ann found a better job in Flagstaff and moved there. It was a little inconvenient because Dillon went to Mark's parents every weekend. They would meet Mary Ann halfway on Friday evenings and Sunday evenings.

It worked out well for Mary Ann because she could work a second job on the weekends. Even though Dillon always returned home with money, presumably from Mark, there were still bills to pay. The money Dillon brought home only went for Dillon's wants and needs. The rest went into a bank account for Dillon's college. Mary Ann refused to use any of Mark's money for herself.

If only William had told her at the beginning, Mary Ann ponders. Although she doesn't think William would hurt anyone, including his wife, she wonders if he didn't tell her out of guilt. I just need time to think this through, so I'll avoid William for a few days.

Chapter 17

Three days go by, and Mary Ann decides she is ready to talk to William. So she sends him a message asking him to come over for coffee. In a few minutes, he is knocking on her door. William walks into the house but won't look at Mary Ann.

"Come into the kitchen, and we can talk," Mary Ann tells him. William follows her into the kitchen and sits down. Lucy runs to meet him. William cheerfully picks her up.

After Mary Ann pours their coffee, she sits the cups on the table and sits across from William.

"William, please look at me." He does. "William, I don't believe you had anything to do with your wife's disappearance or Sam's death. You aren't that type of person. I wish you had told me everything in the beginning."

"I know, Mary Ann, and I'm sorry. Surely you can understand the shame I've felt all these years for not protecting my wife if something bad happened to her."

"There's no way I could ever understand what you and your kids have been through. I'm sorry you went through that. But William, if you and I are to have any kind of relationship, we need honesty and trust."

"I agree. I want to have a relationship with you, Mary Ann. You are the first woman I have ever wanted to get to know and be with. What can I do to make that happen?"

"Is there anything else I should know about you?" Mary Ann asks.

"I've searched my heart and mind and have come up with nothing else of importance to tell you. However, if you ever want to ask questions, I will answer honestly."

"Good, and I'll do the same. Now, can we pick up with where we left off?" Mary Ann asks.

William smiles. "Mary Ann, do you really want to drink that coffee right now?" She shakes her head, takes William's hand, and they head to the bedroom.

Two days later, the police announce they have captured Sam's killer. According to the newspaper, Sam was killed by his drug supplier. Sam had been skimming money from his payments to the supplier. The news came as a relief for William, who had continued to be under the watchful eye of the police.

There were no services for Sam that anyone was aware of. Two weeks later, a For Sale sign appeared on the lawn. A few family members came to the house and removed what they wanted. The house was sold furnished to a couple from Texas. They moved in one month later.

Mary Ann and William's relationship grew strong. William asked Mary Ann to move in with him, but she declined. She wanted to keep her house, knowing she would tire of William and his mechanical sex after a while. The couple traveled on several overnight trips and spent as much time with each other as possible.

Chapter 18

Everything appeared to be going Mary Ann's way until four months later, when she saw a police car parked in William's driveway. She waited until the car left and then hurried to William's house. He didn't answer the door, so Mary Ann let herself in the unlocked door. When she walked in, Mary Ann heard William retching in the bathroom. Several minutes later, he appeared pale, as if he had seen a ghost.

"Oh, my gosh, William! Are you okay? Can I get you anything?" William shakes his head. He sits down on the sofa. Mary Ann goes into the bathroom, returns with a cool washcloth, and wipes his face.

"William, you are so pale and shaking. You don't have a fever, though. What's wrong? I saw the police car. I thought Sam's investigation was over, and you were cleared."

"Mary Ann, it's nothing like that," William whispers. "It's Katie. The police have found Katie," he says before jumping up and going to the bathroom to retch again. Mary Ann follows and has to hold William because he is shaking so badly. When he's finished, he closes the lid on the toilet. Mary Ann helps him sit down. Then she kneels at his feet.

"Katie is alive. She is in Mesa. The police arrested her for shoplifting," William says with great effort. He looks at Mary Ann, and she sees a haunted, terrified look in his eyes.

"Katie told the police she has nowhere to go, so they are bringing her here tomorrow."

"Surely, this is some nightmare we're both going to wake up from," Mary Ann says.

"No, Mary Ann. It's no nightmare. It's the truth." William stands and helps her to her feet. "Let's go back to the living room. I think I'm finished in here."

Once seated on the sofa, Mary Ann asks, "what can I do to help you?"

"I don't know. I know no more information than that. Oh, Mary Ann, I need to call the kids. Look, as much as I care for you, I don't want you drug into this mess. It may be best if we don't see each other until I get all this straightened out."

"I understand," Mary Ann says as tears form in her eyes. "You do whatever you need to do. You know where to find me." She reaches up and removes the necklace William gave her. Mary Ann hands it to him. "Here. Save this for me."

William takes the necklace from her. "I promise to give it back soon, I hope." Then, with tears in his eyes, William caresses Mary Ann's cheek as she stands. Then she walks out of his house.

Early the following day, Mary Ann watches as two vehicles arrive at William's house. A man exits each vehicle and solemnly walks into William's house. Interesting, Mary Ann thinks. William said he had three kids that live close by. Maybe the third one will come later.

At 11:00, Mary Ann peeks out her window as a police car pulls in front of William's house. William and the two men exit the house and stand on the front porch. When the police officer opens the back door, a petite, blond woman gets out of the car. She looks around and then runs to the front porch, throwing her arms around William. William doesn't respond, so the woman backs away and hugs each of the two men, who look very uncomfortable. The police officer takes William aside, and the two talk for several minutes.

Finally, the police car leaves and the four people enter the house. Mary Ann checks throughout the day but never sees William's third child arrive at the home. At 6:00, the two younger men emerge from the house, get into their vehicles, and leave.

"Wow!" Mary Ann says to Lucy. "What interesting conversations must be going on in that house. Well, it's none of my business. William will tell me what he wants me to know."

Chapter 19

Mary Ann swore to herself she wouldn't be the nosy neighbor watching out of her window all the time. But, she couldn't resist looking at William's house the next morning when she went out to get her newspaper. But she noticed William didn't leave for his daily golf game.

Greta is away on a trip, and the new neighbors in Sam's old house don't venture out as early as Mary Ann, so the street is quiet. So Mary Ann takes her newspaper and coffee out to the patio.

When she opens the paper, there is a glaring headline. "Woman Missing Since 1991 Found in Mesa". The article said the woman, Katie (last name withheld), disappeared from Flagstaff in 1991 and had been assumed deceased. However, the woman was arrested for shoplifting in Mesa and was identified by fingerprints after giving the police a false name. The article said they had arrested the woman several times before under the false name. The dollar amount of the shoplifted merchandise under this arrest caused the fingerprint examination. Police returned the woman to her family. They declined further comment because of an ongoing investigation that included federal authorities since the woman was declared deceased by her family in 1998.

Although she didn't doubt what William told her, this confirmed his story and what a story it was. I wonder what type of charges there would be, and if they would involve William, Mary Ann wonders. William must be a mess by now. I wish I could talk to him, but the ball is in his court. She will have to wait for him.

The following morning, there is no more information in the newspaper, which disappoints Mary Ann. So she goes shopping. As she backs out of her garage, Mary Ann catches a movement in her rearview mirror that causes her to slam on her brakes. Walking across the street directly toward her is Katie. Mary Ann rolls down her window as Katie approaches.

"I could have hit you," Mary Ann says to the woman.

"Oh, sorry. I wanted to catch you before you left. I'm Katie and I just got back from an extended vacation. My husband said you were a gracious lady, so I wanted to meet you."

Mary Ann looks forward and thinks, oh dear God. What did I do to deserve this hell? "Hi, Katie. It's nice to meet you. I'm Mary Ann."

"Have you lived here long?"

Mary Ann takes a few seconds to look Katie over. She estimates Katie is one or two years younger than she is. The blond hair appears dyed, and even with the caked-on makeup, the wrinkles around Katie's eyes reveal a woman who hasn't had a tranquil life. "I've only lived here a few months," Mary Ann lies.

"Well, I hope we can be friends," Katie says.

When hell freezes over, Mary Ann thinks. "We'll see," she says. Then Mary Ann looks closer at Katie and almost gets sick to her stomach. "That's a beautiful necklace." Katie is wearing the necklace William gave Mary Ann.

"Isn't it lovely? I found it in William's nightstand. I guess he bought it for me as a surprise. I thought I would just wear it now instead of waiting for him to give it to me. He knows I like cats."

"Does William know you're wearing it?"

Katie touches the necklace. "No."

Mary Ann swallows hard. "Maybe you should put it back before he sees you wearing it, so it will be a surprise when he gives it to you. I must go, Katie, or I'll be late for my appointment."

"Okay. I'll see you later."

Mary Ann barely lets Katie get out of the way before she continues back out. Mary Ann drives out of the neighborhood and has to pull over and cry. Katie is wearing my necklace. Why didn't William hide it? I'll never wear it again, even if William gives it back.

Drowning her hurt and anger in shopping, Mary Ann doesn't get home until after dark. Then she takes a bottle of wine and a glass to her patio and stays until the bottle is empty.

Greta returns from her trip the following day. She and Mary Ann spend the afternoon together, catching up on everything happening across the street. Greta can tell Mary Ann is upset and tries to console her, but to no avail.

"Greta, I need to get away for a few days. Would you mind taking care of Lucy?"

"Of course not, Mary Ann. You take as long as you need."

"Thanks, I'll let you know."

After Greta leaves, Mary Ann looks up her favorite cabin in Eureka Springs and is thrilled to find it is available the following week. She books the cabin for an entire week. Then, Mary Ann books her flights and vehicle. She can leave the day after tomorrow and calls Greta.

Chapter 20

Mary Ann spends the week away from home, refusing to think about William and remembering her time with Mark. She thinks about her son, Dillon, a lot, though.

Mary Ann hasn't seen Dillon since he went off to college. Dillon was intelligent and went to college in California on a baseball scholarship. Every time Mary Ann wanted to see Dillon, he had a baseball game, practice, playoffs, or exams. It didn't matter what time of year Mary Ann wanted to go. Dillon never came home. Mary Ann knew Mark moved to California to be close to his son. At least Dillon had a parent's guidance.

At first, she and Dillon talked twice a week, but it tapered off. Then they didn't talk at all. Mary Ann wasn't invited to his graduation. Just like his father, Mary Ann thinks. Just left me with no explanation. I can't help but wonder if Mark has something to do with it. Surely Mark wouldn't be that vindictive. I just don't know. Regardless, I'm glad Dillon had his dad.

A week after Mary Ann returns, there's a knock on the door. Hoping it is William, she's disappointed to find Katie.

"Hello, Katie."

"Hi, Mary Ann," Katie says, all bouncy and happy. "Would you like to come over for coffee? I asked William about you, and he said you were a gracious lady."

"Thanks, Katie, but I'm in the middle of something." Mary Ann notices the necklace is still around Katie's neck.

"That's okay. William said you were a very private person. Maybe some other time. I'm trying to get William out of the house more. I want to go to the pool so bad."

"Then you should go, Katie. Don't let William keep you from things you want to do."

"I'm limited in what I can do. I can't drive, so I have to rely on William. Oh, well. Take care, Mary Ann." Katie turns and returns home.

"There's no way I'll ever have coffee with you and William," Mary Ann says aloud.

Several months pass by. Mary Ann lives her life as if she never met William. She takes two trips abroad and ignores the house across the street. Katie never visits again. Twice, Mary Ann ran into William and Katie in the hardware store. Both times, Katie was her usual happy self. She told Mary Ann the first time that William was letting her drive even though she doesn't have a license. The last time Mary Ann saw them, she noticed the necklace was gone.

William, however, looks drawn and older. He won't look at Mary Ann. When Katie and William walk past Mary Ann, he deliberately brushes her hand, grabs it for a second, and squeezes it. It causes Mary Ann's heart to constrict with grief over the loss of her friend.

Mary Ann and William had booked a cruise before Katie showed up. Presuming William forgot Mary Ann goes alone. A stranger knocks on her door the day after she returns.

The stranger identifies himself as a private investigator hired by William's children to find information about their mother after she left them. Mary Ann has no answers to the man's questions. She tells him what William told her and William's reaction to learning about his wife's return. The man leaves.

Chapter 21

Three weeks after Mary Ann returns from her cruise, William sends her a message asking if he can come to her house. Of course, she replies. William shows up a few minutes later. He walks in and sits down on the sofa.

"Mary Ann," he begins. "The story about Katie is coming out in tomorrow's newspaper, but I wanted you to hear it first from me. Everything I'm going to tell you has been verified by the police and the private investigator my kids hired. What the newspaper prints is up to them."

Mary Ann sits down across from William and nods.

"It seems Katie was unhappy with me and the burden of three kids. Plus, she was bored. Katie was a little wild before I met her. My oldest son isn't my son. I married Katie before she had him and gave him my last name."

Mary Ann senses a lot of heartbreak in William's voice.

"Anyway, while she was working at the real estate office, a long-time friend of her late brother came in looking for a house. Apparently, this man promised the brother that he would look after

Katie if anything should ever happen to her brother. Katie and the man hadn't seen each other in a while."

William pauses briefly and then continues. "Katie wanted away from the kids and me. So she came up with the idea to tell this man, Mark, that I was abusing her. So Mark, bound by his promise to her brother, helped her escape. That's why her car was abandoned with her purse and keys. Katie wanted to make a new start. This Mark had bought a house in another town and hid Katie there for a couple of weeks."

Mary Ann shakes her head and says, "wow. Then what happened?"

"This Mark guy told her he would provide her a place to live and feed her, but she needed to get a job. The only place Katie could get one with no questions was a bar and work for tips. So she got a job, and in three months, she was pregnant. Katie wouldn't tell who the baby's father was. Mark wasn't happy, but he told her their arrangement would stay the same, but Katie had to take care of the baby."

"This is some story," Mary Ann says.

"Yeah, and it gets better," William says with a smirk. "Katie had the baby and kept working at the bar. A year later, she was pregnant again. She wouldn't name that father then either. Mark owns a successful heating and air conditioning company, so he has money. He bought a different house with a cottage behind his house for Katie. Good thing, too, because she got pregnant again a year after the second baby was born."

Mary Ann looks at William, astonished. "I bet she didn't name that father either, did she?"

"Of course not. Mark let Katie and the kids live in the cottage until he discovered she was shoplifting. Katie didn't steal baby stuff either. She stole things she could sell on the internet. Even though Mark was supporting her, Katie said she needed more money than she made at the bar."

"Mark kicked Katie and three kids out about ten years ago. According to Katie, he told her he promised her brother to look after her, but her stealing was more than he could take," William says.

"Well, I can understand that, but with three kids, it must have been hard for Katie," Mary Ann states.

"Mark told the police he hadn't heard from Katie until two months ago. Then she told him she needed money and had a necklace to sell."

"My necklace," Mary Ann whispers. "I noticed Katie wasn't wearing it the last time I saw her."

William looks at Mary Ann with tears in his eyes. "I'm sorry, Mary Ann. I didn't give it to her, I swear."

"I know. Katie told me she found it in your nightstand by the bed."

William nods. "Katie told me someone stole it from her at the food store one day when I let her go alone. So I reported it stolen and there's a police report for it. Katie thought Mark would take it to a pawnshop and sell it. He didn't, though. He had it appraised and found it was very expensive. So Mark asked Katie about it. She told him it was a gift. Mark told her he would give her $2,000 and keep it for her. He had it in his safe. The police have it now."

"What a mess," Mary Ann says. "So what now?"

"Well, they investigated me for insurance fraud for having Katie declared dead. She had no life insurance, so they cleared me of that. They charged Mark with possession of stolen property. His lawyer thinks they will throw it out because Katie told Mark it was a gift, which she admitted to. Katie is now in jail."

"What is Katie in jail for?" Mary Ann asks.

"Just about everything," William replies. "Shoplifting, stealing the necklace, not paying income taxes on the tips she made, and selling stolen property. There's more, but I don't remember it all. Katie wanted me to hire a lawyer for her, but I refused. The district attorney says she will go to prison for several years."

"What about her kids?"

"They are grown now with their own families. The oldest is twenty-eight. They have washed their hands of her."

"What about your kids?" Mary Ann asks thoughtfully.

William laughs. "Two of my kids were there when the police brought her to the house. They listened to her story, which wasn't as true as the one I just told you. My daughter refused to see Katie."

William glances at Mary Ann with a serious look. "Now, we need to talk about us."

"Us?" Mary Ann says, like William has grown two heads.

"Yes, us. Mary Ann, I still have feelings for you. I never touched Katie while she was at the house. I swear. She tried twice, but I was adamant about not having a relationship of any kind with her. I told her the only reason she was at my house was that she said she had nowhere to go. I told her to get everything straightened out so she could get an actual job and move out as soon as possible. But she got arrested before she could."

Mary Ann watches William's eyes and can tell he is being truthful.

"Mary Ann, I want us to be together. Not like we were before, but more. I've missed you so much."

"William," she begins. "I've missed you, too, as a friend and companion. But things can never be as they were. There's too much water under the bridge."

William looks at the floor and asks, "have you found someone else?"

"No, but I've moved on with my life. It's time you do the same."

"I understand," William says quietly, standing. "Good luck, Mary Ann. I'll see myself out." With those words, William is gone from her life.

Mary Ann sits in the chair, thinking about the story William just told her. I knew there was something about Katie. I'm glad I didn't agree to be her friend. I would have been drawn into her web of lies, too. Mary Ann picks up a meowing Lucy and holds her tight. "Well, girl, it's the two of us. We'll make it just fine like we always have," Mary Ann says aloud. Lucy agrees with loud purring.

Chapter 22

Mary Ann gets her newspaper the following day expecting to see the same story William told her yesterday. But instead, as she sits on the patio and opens the paper, it is a picture, not the story, that jumps out at her. First, there is a picture of Katie, but there is also a picture of a man identified as Mark Green from Scottsdale.

Mary Ann stares at the picture. Unfortunately, it isn't a good picture because it is grainy and taken at a distance. The man sure looks like her husband, but it is hard to tell.

Mary Ann reads the story slowly, glancing up at the picture repeatedly. The report says Mark Green is scheduled to appear before a judge this afternoon at 1:00. Mary Ann looks at her phone. That's four hours from now. Oh well, good luck Mark Green.

Mary Ann continues with her morning, but she knows in her heart that she has to go to the hearing. She has to find out if it is indeed her husband that is tied up in this mess named Katie.

Mary Ann takes a shower, fixes her hair and makeup, and dresses in a business casual dress. The dress hasn't been worn for a while and is a little tight. Mary Ann finds her Spanx to help her fit into the dress better. Next, she digs her black pumps from the back of her closet. I know it's not my husband, but if it is and he sees me, I want him to know what he's missed all these years. After one more inspection in the mirror, Mary Ann heads to the courthouse.

Several people are waiting to get into the courtroom when Mary Ann arrives at the courthouse. Finally, the doors open, and everyone is let inside. Mary Ann sits at the back, puts her dark sunglasses on, and waits.

1:00 arrives, and Mark and his attorney walk into the courtroom. Mary Ann nearly faints. It is her husband. His hair is salt and pepper and is longer than he ever wore it. It touches his collar now. Mark is freshly shaven. His prominent nose and strong jawline still accentuate his face. Mary Ann can tell instantly his suit is expensive and fits his body perfectly. Mark reaches to shake hands with someone, and she sees the powerful muscles across his back.

Mary Ann's heart beats faster than it has since Mark left. A warmth runs through her body directly to an area Mark knew intimately at one time. Mary Ann blushes at the feelings the sight of Mark has stirred inside her. Dammit, it's been over forty years, and the sight of that man still has that effect on me, Mary Ann thinks.

At that moment, the judge enters the courtroom. The proceedings begin, but Mary Ann cannot concentrate. She stares at the back of Mark's head. She watches every move he makes. When he turns his head and smiles at his attorney, Mary Ann's breath catches. She remembers Mark's 1,000-watt smile, and tears come to her eyes.

Mary Ann returns to reality in time to realize the judge has thrown Mark's case out. It is over. Mary Ann stands to make her way outside quickly, but there are too many people in her row of seats blocking her in. She feels something tugging at her. Mary Ann looks up just as Mark turns around. He looks directly at her. He stares for a few seconds and then blesses her with his 1,000-watt smile.

"Oh dear Lord, he recognizes me," Mary Ann whispers. She pushes people along, trying to get out as soon as possible. All she wants to do is get to her car and get home. Panic overtakes her. Finally, she is outside. She stops momentarily to take a deep breath before hurrying to her car. But then, the inevitable happens. She feels a hand on her elbow, and a tsunami runs through her body and soul.

"Kitten!"

Mary Ann takes another deep breath and turns toward HIM. "Mark."

"Kitten, what are you doing here?"

"Well, this has been such a fascinating story, and I saw the picture in the newspaper. So I had to find out if it was really you in the middle of the fiasco. Would you kindly let go of my elbow?"

"I'm sorry," Mark says. "Let's move over here out of the crowd." His hand is still on Mary Ann's elbow, and he guides her down the courthouse steps and onto the less crowded sidewalk, but he still doesn't release her.

"Mark, my elbow."

Mark removes his hand from her elbow. He reaches up with both hands and removes Mary Ann's sunglasses. "My God! You are still so beautiful." Mark uses one hand to caress her cheek.

"Mark, please," Mary Ann whispers. Her heart silently begging him not to touch her anymore.

"Kitten, please look at me," Mark whispers, standing so close Mary Ann can smell his cologne. The cologne is her favorite—the one she always gave him for special occasions. Mark doesn't move his hand. Instead, his fingers linger on her cheek.

Mary Ann drifts her eyes up to his. Those beautiful green eyes that suck her in and drown her. She flashes back to her seventeenth birthday when Mark first made love to her. His eyes and hands were on her body. Each look and each touch created a fire inside her that not even time has diminished. She looks down quickly, hoping Mark doesn't see her fire for him in her eyes.

"It's good to see you, Kitten. Do you have time for a cup of coffee?"

Mary Ann laughs. "You're asking me to have coffee with you after not seeing you for forty years? I don't think so, and please, don't call me Kitten."

"You have every right to be bitter. Okay, then if not coffee, come to my house tomorrow night. Dillon and Devon will be there. Dillon says he has some exciting news."

"No, Mark."

Mark finally moves his hand from Mary Ann's cheek and reaches into his pocket. He pulls out a business card and a pen. He writes something down on the back of the card and hands it to her.

"Here's my address and phone number if you change your mind. I need to get back to work. It's wonderful to see my wife again," Mark says. Then he leans down and kisses Mary Ann's lips softly. He turns and walks away before she can react.

Mary Ann instinctively touches her lips. Then she shoves the card in her purse and practically runs to her SUV, trying to beat the tears. Once in the car, Mary Ann leans her head on the steering wheel and sobs hard. She cries out of hurt for Mark leaving her. She cries out of anger because her heart and body have betrayed her after all these years. But, most of all, Mary Ann cries because she still loves Mark with everything she has.

When the sobbing subsides, Mary Ann takes Mark's card from her purse, reads it, and starts to throw it out the window. Then an idea comes to her. "Okay, Mark. I'll show up at your house tomorrow night, but not for the reason you think," Mary Ann says aloud with hostility. She stuffs the card back into her purse and drives to her bank.

Once at the bank, Mary Ann goes inside and closes the account with all the money Mark has sent her all these years. Then she gets a cashier's check made payable to Mark. Since she didn't need the money for Dillon's college, the amount surprises Mary Ann. She leaves the bank and heads home to work on her plan.

Chapter 23

Mary Ann is dressed and ready to leave for Mark's house by 5:30 pm. According to the GPS on her phone, the drive should take approximately forty-five minutes. That would put her there between 6:15 and 6:45, depending on traffic.

"Showtime," Mary Ann tells Lucy as she cuddles her. "You go to bed. There're be plenty of time to play when I get home. Sitting the cat on the floor, Mary Ann picks up her purse and the envelope containing the cashier's check. She checks herself in the mirror one more time and heads to her car.

Earlier, Mary Ann decided since this would not be a social call, there was no point in dressing up. She did that yesterday. So now she is dressed in leggings, a t-shirt, and tennis shoes.

As she pulls into Mark's driveway, Mary Ann is impressed with his house. Well, he seems to do well for himself. She parks next to a BMW and an Audi and smiles. Someone likes to show off, she thinks. She gets out of the SUV, walks up the sidewalk, and rings the doorbell.

In a few seconds, Mark opens the door. Seeing Mary Ann, he gives her his signature 1,000-watt smile. "Kitten, I was hoping you'd come."

Mary Ann does not comment but gives Mark a stern look because he called her Kitten after she told him not to. As she steps into the house, Mary Ann sees Dillon sitting on the sofa with another man. The man immediately gets up, coming toward her.

"You must be Mrs. Green. I'm Devon," the man says. Mary Ann gives him a slight smile and turns her cold eyes to Dillon, who is watching her intently.

"Kitten, we've been waiting for you. Dillon and Devon say they have some exciting news to share," Mark says.

"That's not why I'm here. Now that I know where you are, I can give you this," Mary Ann says with a coldness that chills the air. She hands the envelope to Mark, turns, and walks out of the house.

Mary Ann gets into her SUV quickly, so Mark won't have time to stop her. She left the engine running so she could leave in a hurry. Mary Ann takes a deep breath as she pulls onto the street. "The End!" she yells inside the car. "Well, almost, but it's a beginning."

Once home, Mary Ann changes into a sexy, very low-cut camisole and shorts and climbs into bed with Lucy. First, Mary Ann tells the cat what happened. Then they play until bedtime, and Mary Ann finally has a dreamless sleep.

Chapter 24

Mary Ann is walking into the living room when she hears a car in her driveway. She peeks out the window, not surprised to see it is Mark. She looks down. She is still dressed in her nightclothes. Oh, what the heck, Mary Ann thinks. Mark has seen me in less than this.

The doorbell rings, and she waits a minute before opening the door.

"Wow! Please tell me you don't go get the paper dressed like that every morning," Mark says, flashing his 1,000-watt smile.

"What took you so long to get here?" Mary Ann asks, ignoring Mark's comment.

"Well, I had to find out where you lived first. Can I come in?"

Mary Ann motions him inside and takes the newspaper from him. Mark follows her into the living room, where she tosses the paper on the sofa.

"Mark, what are you doing here?"

"We need to talk."

"I don't think there is anything to talk about after all these years, do you?"

"Yes, we have a great deal to talk about, or at least, I do."

Mary Ann rolls her eyes at him. "Look, I was about to make breakfast. Have you eaten?" Mark shakes his head, eyeing her up and down. "Well, come in the kitchen, and we'll eat, but I have one condition. Let's eat like normal people and have a decent conversation."

"I can do that. What can I do to help?"

Mark follows Mary Ann into the kitchen. "You can put the coffee on."

Mark goes to the coffeemaker and starts the process. Mary Ann knows he's watching her, so she opens the fridge and bends over more than necessary to retrieve the bacon and eggs. "I only have canned biscuits. Is that okay? I guess I should ask if you have any dietary restrictions these days."

"I can eat just about anything, and canned biscuits are fine. What else can I do?"

"Would you turn the oven on 350 degrees?"

Mark turns the oven on and opens cabinets, looking for coffee cups. "Do you still take your coffee black, Mary Ann?"

"Yes." She walks around him to get a frying pan and returns to the cooktop. She opens the package of bacon and places several pieces in the pan to fry. "Do you want your eggs over easy like you used to or scrambled?"

"Over easy, please. I'm surprised you remember," Mark says.

"Oh, you'd be surprised what I remember, but general conversation, okay?"

"Sure, Kitten." Mary Ann turns and gives Mark a frown, which he ignores. He opens the cabinets and finds everything he needs to set the table.

"Mark, there's orange and apple juice in the fridge. Pick out what you want. There's strawberry jam and orange marmalade in there as well."

Mark walks over to the fridge, brushing up against Mary Ann's back as he does. He selects apple juice and orange marmalade and sets those items on the counter. Mark also gets the butter while he has the door open.

Mary Ann wishes he wouldn't touch her. I can't handle it, she says to herself.

"I think that's everything," Mark says.

"Great. Would you pour us a cup of coffee while I work here? You can sit down and relax. It won't be long."

Mark pours the coffee. He sets a cup beside where Mary Ann is cooking, takes his cup to the table, and sits down.

"This is a nice place, Mary Ann. The neighborhood seems quiet."

"It is nice and quiet. Everyone's retired. About one-half of the residents are active, and the others are not. My neighbor next door was murdered a few months ago, but it happened elsewhere."

"That's a little scary. Did they catch the killer?"

"Yes, his drug dealer killed him. My neighbor was the resident painkiller and other prescription medication supplier for the neighborhood." Mary Ann puts the biscuits into the oven, feeling Mark's eyes watching her every move.

"That's a little scary," Mark says.

"Not really, since it happened elsewhere. I guess nothing exciting like that goes on in your neighborhood."

"We are having a rash of burglaries right now. I've been lucky so far. The police think it is a group, so they have increased patrols. The thieves drive a van and back into driveways and make it look like they are some type of repair service."

Mary Ann sits the bacon on the table and starts work on the eggs. The oven timer goes off, and Mark gets up to get the biscuits from the oven. Mary Ann collects his plate and places three perfectly cooked eggs on it. Then she puts one on her plate.

"Let's eat," Mary Ann says, sitting down.

Mark refills their cups and sits down across from her. "Mary Ann, this looks delicious. The eggs are perfect."

Just as Mary Ann requested, she and Mark discuss general topics while eating. Like any couple, they discuss the weather, politics, and local events.

When they finish, Mary Ann tells Mark just to leave everything. She will clean up later, but right now, she is going to take a shower and dress. Mark should make himself at home. Instead, Mark cleans the kitchen while Mary Ann is in the shower.

When Mary Ann finishes her shower, she enters the bedroom wrapped in a towel. She's surprised to find Mark sitting on her bed waiting for her. "Do you think you could give me a few minutes of privacy so I can dress?"

"No, I have something else in mind." Mark stands and pulls back the bedcovers. "Get into bed."

"You've got to be kidding me?" Mary Ann asks, anger flashing in her eyes.

"I'm not kidding. It's not what you think, I promise," Mark replies, staring into her angry eyes. "Just do it. Please."

Mary Ann stomps over to her side of the king-sized bed. "Can you at least turn around?" Mark rolls his eyes and turns his back to her. Mary Ann drops the towel, climbs into bed, and pulls the covers up to her neck. "Okay, I'm in."

Mark walks to the opposite side of the bed and removes his shoes. "Now, I'm going to talk, and you'll listen. No questions until the end. Understand?"

Mary Ann nods, wondering what Mark's up to. She glances into his eyes but does not find any sign of desire in them. Instead, she only sees a warm glow in those beautiful green eyes.

Mark cautiously lies down beside Mary Ann. He lies on his side with his head propped on his hand, supported by his bent elbow. Mark looks down at her, lying flat on her back, and smirks. Then, suddenly, he reaches for the bed covers under Mary Ann's neck and jerks them down below her feet. Mark hears her sharp breath intake as Mary Ann realizes what had just happened.

"Now, that's better," Mark says in a low voice. He smiles at Mary Ann.

Mary Ann looks into those green eyes and says defiantly, "now what? Are you pleased to see me naked, or will you laugh?"

"Mary Ann, I said no questions. What part of that did you not understand?" Mark shakes his head and inspects her body from her head to her toes. "You are just as beautiful now as you were the day I married you," he whispers. Mary Ann opens her mouth to comment, but Mark places a finger on her lips to stop her. "Just listen, okay?" Mary Ann nods and closes her eyes to hide her embarrassment.

Mark removes his finger from her lips. He takes a deep breath and begins his story. "I began watching you sleep on our wedding night, and I watched you every night. Sometimes it was right after you fell asleep. Sometimes it was the middle of the night when I would wake up, and sometimes before the alarm would go off. Every night I watched, amazed that this beautiful, caring woman fell in love with me and married me. Yes, you were pregnant, but you didn't have to marry me and didn't have to love me. I thanked God every night for you then and still do."

Mary Ann slowly opens her eyes. Mark is staring at her face. She notices tears form in his eyes, which he blinks away.

"If you remember, I insisted on us sleeping naked with a night light. I wanted to see you. All of you and commit every inch of you to memory. I also wanted to watch and experience your body's changes as our baby grew inside you."

Now Mary Ann's eyes fill with tears, remembering sleeping naked in Mark's arms and how much she loved every minute.

"Of course, it didn't take long for the changes to begin, but I watched every night. First, you gained a little weight. Then, your beautiful breasts changed. They grew larger and fuller, preparing to produce the milk for our baby. Your nipples changed so our baby would have more to suckle on."

Mary Ann listens, fascinated. She knew Mark noticed changes in her body, but she always felt it had to do with making love more than the baby. She looks into Mark's eyes and sees a warm glow. He smiles at her and continues.

"I watched your feet and ankles swell to where you couldn't wear anything but flip-flops or house shoes. Then your belly grew. First, it was just a little plumpness around your middle, and then it got larger. It amazed me that a baby was growing inside you. Our baby that we made together. I would lie there next to you and wish I could see inside you to watch the baby grow." Mark stops momentarily and holds a deep breath. Mary Ann senses the emotions he is feeling. Mark lays his hand on her stomach, reliving his memories. She watches him but doesn't move his hand.

"When the baby started moving, it seemed so active. I would lie there and watch and wonder how you could sleep. Then, there were nights I would just lie next to you with my hand on your belly, feeling those little kicks and turns. Sometimes, I would whisper to it to sleep so as not to wake mommy." Mark takes another deep breath and continues.

"I hated to leave you every day. I was so afraid the baby would come, and I would miss out. I wanted so bad to be there with you. Fortunately, our little bundle of joy started his fight to get out early evening. You were calm, and I was so excited. I forgot to call everyone, so no one was at the hospital for a while but us." Mark smiles and shakes his head.

"I remember," Mary Ann speaks up. "Between labor pains, you had to go out to make the calls. Do you remember you had to come in several times and ask me the phone numbers for our parents? You would forget by the time you got back out into the hallway."

Mark smiles. "Yeah, I remember. That nurse finally took pity on me and wrote them down." He looks into Mary Ann's eyes, happy to see her smile. Mark begins stroking her hair and moves a lock behind Mary Ann's ear.

"You were in so much pain, Kitten. It broke my heart to watch you as I held your hand. Then, the doctor called me to get ready. I watched as your body opened up, and the top of that tiny head emerged. Then more and more came until he was out. Our little baby was a boy. The doctor did what he needed to and then handed him to me. That little boy looked me straight in the eyes as I laid him on you."

"It was a crazy moment because all three of us were crying," Mary Ann adds, tears filling her eyes. She reaches up and gently touches Mark's cheek.

Mark nods as tears fill his eyes again. "Our perfect little family. I had never felt so much love in my heart as I did at that moment. I thought I was going to explode."

Mary Ann remembers she is naked and moves her hand from Mark's face to pull the covers over her.

"I'm not finished yet," Mark states as he grabs her hand to stop her.

"Oh, sorry."

"After the baby was born, I still watched you every night. Your body went through so much with the baby growing inside you and then having the baby. I wish I could have helped in some way."

"Mark, you helped. You were so loving and kind. I couldn't have asked for a better husband than you." Mary Ann strokes his cheek and runs her fingers through his hair, noticing a familiar feeling inside her she hadn't felt in years.

"I don't feel I did enough, though. I watched your breasts create more and more milk for our baby."

"Yeah, that was before breast pumps, and you helped me out with that when it was needed."

"I enjoyed that," Mark says, looking into Mary Ann's eyes with a devilish look.

Mary Ann laughs. "I know you did."

"You worked so hard to get your body back into shape. Your belly decreased in size. I remember all those times I rubbed scar cream on your belly."

Mary Ann rubs her stomach and states, "well, it helped little."

Mark strokes his hand over her stomach, saying, "it looks great." Then he moves his hand away, not wanting to make her uncomfortable. Next, Mark reaches down and pulls the cover over Mary Ann. He stares into her blue-gray eyes with a deep intensity Mary Ann feels in her soul.

"Kitten, we were so happy. We had little money, but you could stay home with Dillon for a while. I remember, after dinner, we would read and play with him until his bedtime."

"We didn't own a TV. So Dillon was our entertainment." Mary Ann smiles at the memories.

"You were so kind to let me go out once a week with Ross and let off steam. You never said you wanted to go out with your friends or get away from the house."

"Mark, I didn't need that. You did. You worked all day and many weekends. Your nights were spent with Dillon and me. You needed that time away. I noticed your times with Ross changed from once a week to every two weeks. Then it became once a month. I hope I didn't make you feel guilty."

"No, Kitten. You didn't. Things changed. My priorities changed. You and Dillon were my life. Ross always wanted to drink and then ride our motorcycles. I stopped drinking because I didn't want something to happen to me, and you and Dillon would be left with medical bills or funeral expenses."

"What happened, Mark? We were so happy for three years or, at least, I thought we were." Mary Ann feels the shift in Mark and a coldness creep up the back of her neck. Yet, she wants to know and needs to know, even if it is years too late.

Chapter 25

Mark turns over and lies on his back, looking at the ceiling, so Mary Ann turns on her side to face him. "Mark, I deserve to know what happened to us since you just left me without saying a word."

He glances at Mary Ann. "I know you do, and you shouldn't have had to wait this long for an explanation, but I just couldn't bring myself to tell you. I was too ashamed."

"Will you tell me now?" she whispers.

Mark stares into Mary Ann's eyes for what seems like a very long time. She sees hurt and fear in his eyes before turning his face back to the ceiling.

"I've told no one this. Well, that's not true. I have spent years with therapists and bared my heart and soul to them. All of them told me I should have shared this with you from the beginning, but I just couldn't do it. I guess I'm finally healed enough to tell you."

Mark takes a big, deep breath and holds it for several seconds. "Okay, here goes. Ross and I had been at a club the night he died. You know that."

Mary Ann nods. She feels this will be very hard for Mark, so she lays her hand on his chest, feeling his rapid heartbeat. Mark glances down at her hand but doesn't move it away. Instead, he reaches for her hand with his and squeezes Mary Ann's hand tightly.

"Ross had several drinks that night despite my repeated requests to slow down. He called me weak and told me I wasn't any fun anymore since the baby was born and I had stopped drinking. We had words, and he stomped out of the club. Of course, I followed him and tried to stop him from getting on his motorcycle. He shoved me down and got on, and raced off. I followed him, trying to catch up with him. The light turned red, and I stopped. Ross didn't, and he got hit. I jumped off my bike and ran to him. He died in my arms."

"I'm so sorry, Mark. I did not know you were holding him when he died," Mary Ann says, tears filling her eyes.

"It was hard. Hard because we had words, and I couldn't stop Ross from getting on his bike. For many years, I thought maybe that should have been me that got killed instead of Mark. Anyway, I felt so guilty and angry. I started drinking heavily, but you already know that because you had to get a job to help pay the bills."

"I remember very well, but I didn't know why you started drinking again. But then, you stayed out all night and wouldn't come home for a few days."

"I started using drugs to help with the pain and anger I was feeling. At first, it was pot, and when that didn't work anymore, I moved to the more brutal stuff. I was fighting with anyone that wanted to fight. I threw things and tore things apart. I tore up the motorcycle shop and got fired."

"Mark, why didn't you talk to me? Why didn't you tell me? Maybe we could have worked it out."

"It wasn't your problem, Kitten. It was mine."

"That's where you were wrong. We were married. Your problems were my problems."

Mark interrupts Mary Ann. "Let me continue, please. One day, I was at a bar at the other end of town. I got into a fight and beat the guy pretty badly. I broke my hand. It was then I decided I couldn't go home to you because I was afraid I would get angry and hurt you." Tears have rolled down Mark's checks. "I knew I wouldn't hurt Dillon since he was a baby, but I could hurt you, the beautiful, loving woman that married me. I couldn't take a chance on losing my temper and hurting you. I didn't want to bruise your beautiful body. I would have killed myself if I had done that."

Mary Ann stares at Mark in utter disbelief. Unfazed by his tears, she looks at him with loathing. "So you just quit on me and our marriage. All these years, I have wondered what I did wrong." Her voice rises louder and louder. "I thought you found another woman and didn't love me anymore. I thought I was the problem. How dare you do that to me? How dare you, your sorry bastard?" She jumps out of bed, grabs her robe from the foot of the bed, and runs to the bathroom sobbing.

Mark watches her, astonished. She thought it was her all this time; he ponders. Mark listens to the uncontrollable sobbing coming from the bathroom and doesn't know what to do. Mary Ann never blamed him. She blamed herself. He has to make her understand.

The problem is, he is still in love with her. Mark knows he never stopped, and damn, lying in bed next to her brought back so many beautiful memories, especially with his wife naked. He had been with other women years after he left her, but he loved none of them. Mark just used them and never long-term because he didn't want the hassle of them getting too close to him.

The sobbing in the bathroom continues, and Mark's heart is breaking. He looks at the clock and realizes it is lunchtime. Kitten probably won't eat, but he'll make something and think. Mark gets out of bed and heads to the kitchen.

Mary Ann's tears are out of anger more than hurt. All these years, she blamed herself when Mark was to blame for leaving her and never giving her the divorce she wanted so she could move on. Damn him! He was so selfish and waited all these years to tell her. He destroyed her when he left, and now he's done it again with his revelations.

Her sobbing subsides, but her anger lingers on. She peeks out the bathroom door and sees Mark isn't in the bedroom. Mary Ann quietly begins dressing, hoping Mark has left, but the aroma of bacon cooking hits her nose. That ass is cooking bacon. Mary Ann considers it is lunchtime, but I don't think I can eat. She finishes dressing, takes a deep breath, and goes into the kitchen.

Chapter 26

When Mary Ann walks into the kitchen, Mark's back is toward her. He is slicing tomatoes. "You're hungry?" she asks.

"A little," Mark answers. "Are you?"

"You're kidding, right?"

"No, I'm not. Besides, I have more to tell you if you want to listen. I have all day."

"I'm not sure I can take anymore." Mary Ann reaches into a cabinet, grabs the ibuprofen, and gets a glass of water. She takes two pills out, returning the bottle to the cabinet. Then Mary Ann takes the pills and sits down at the table.

"Have you got a headache?" Mark asks in a concerned voice.

"Wouldn't you if you just found out the last forty years of your life were a lie?"

"I guess so. Do you want a sandwich or not?"

Mary Ann watches Mark walk to the fridge and get the lettuce and mayo. "Yeah, go ahead and make me one. I can always save it for later. So you have more to tell? Start talking so you can leave and never let me see you again."

"I will when I finish the sandwiches. After that, I have a proposition for you."

"Well, that should be interesting, like anything matters after all this time."

Mark looks over his shoulder at Mary Ann. Her eyes are swollen, her nose is red, and her face is blotchy. "You really sound bitter."

"I suppose you will tell me I have nothing to be bitter about. So after all these years, you come waltzing in here with your confession, and I should be happy? Happy to see you? Happy to get everything out in the open? Happy we're still married? Well, think again."

Mark turns around and faces her. "No, Mary Ann. It's not like that at all. I left you, and I'm very sorry, but I chose to hurt you emotionally rather than physically. You would have really hated me then."

"Do you really think you would have hurt me physically?"

"I do. Even if it were just bruises from grabbing your arms, I couldn't take leaving any marks on you."

"But you left marks on my body. There're called stretch marks."

"I refuse to think of those as marks, and I don't believe you consider them marks either. Dillon was conceived in a passionate moment when we expressed our love for each other. I can't change what I did, and honestly, I would make the same decision again if I thought I might hurt you." Mark turns his back to Mary Ann and makes the sandwiches.

She watches Mark's back and ponders what he just said. The kitchen is silent except for the noise Mark makes. He finishes with the sandwiches and turns around with a plate in each hand. He hands Mary Ann her plate.

"Mary Ann, are you good with water, or would you like something else? I'm having coffee."

"I'm good with water. It looks like you cleaned up after breakfast."

Mark sits his plate on the table and turns to fill his coffee cup. "I did while you were in the shower."

"Well, thank you, and thanks for the sandwich."

"You're welcome. I'll clean this mess up later, too." Mark sits across the table from Mary Ann and takes a big bite out of his sandwich. "You need to eat," he says to her.

"Would you like some chips, Mark? There are potato chips in the cabinet." Mary Ann points to the cabinet to Mark's left. He gets up, grabs the chips, and then opens the bag, dumping a handful on his plate. Mark offers Mary Ann the bag, but she shakes her head. "Well, Mark, please continue with your story. I'm all ears," she says sarcastically.

Mark looks over the table at her and shakes his head before beginning. "Well, to pick up where I left off. I broke my hand and went to the Emergency Room. The doctor that treated me also saw after Ross when he died. Not knowing any of my family or you, he called Ross' dad."

"Why didn't you give him my number? Oh wait, you had already decided you didn't want me anymore."

"Can I please just tell the story?" Mark says, rolling his eyes.

"Please continue. I'm sure this will be memorable," Mary Ann quips.

"Ross' dad came to the hospital. He said he heard I was having a hard time with Ross' death, but he did not know it was as bad as it was. I was higher than a kite on something, drunk, hadn't bathed in days, and didn't care. He offered to drive me home, but I said I didn't have a home anymore, so he took me to his house. He bathed me and put me to bed while Ross' mother went and bought me some clothes."

Mark takes another bite of his sandwich and takes a moment to chew before continuing. The smell of bacon gets to Mary Ann, and she takes a small bite of her sandwich.

Mark watches her. "Just eat. I didn't poison the damn thing. Well, I guess I slept for a good day or so. I woke up with chills and shakes, but instead of giving me any alcohol to drink, Ross' dad dressed me and put me in his car. He drove for I don't know how long. Finally, he pulled into a treatment center. I refused to get out of the car, so he had two orderlies physically remove me from the car and take me inside. I was told Ross' dad just drove off."

Mary Ann takes a big bite of her sandwich and waits for Mark to continue his story.

"First, they had to detox me. That took several days because I had so much stuff in my body. Once that was over, they started therapy. I fought the therapy at first. I fought it hard, but Ross' father came to see me and told me my son needed me. He said he knew what kind of home I grew up in, so I should know better than anyone about a boy needing his father. That hit me in the gut, and I started taking the therapy seriously."

"Okay," Mary Ann says. "I have to ask. Where does Dillon fit in? I dropped him off at your parents' house every weekend, assuming he was with you."

"I swear I never drank or did drugs while I was around Dillon. I was never alone with him. My parents saw to that. He was still small, so entertaining him took little effort. My mom or dad always drove if we went for ice cream or anything."

"Thank you for being so concerned about him during that time," Mary Ann says with spite.

"Now, I didn't see him while I was at the treatment center, so when you dropped him off, he was with my mom and dad. Didn't you ever ask them about me?"

"No, why should I? You left me, remember? I was too busy working two jobs and caring for our son."

For the first time, Mark feels anger toward Mary Ann and says, "oh, sorry. I forgot you're the martyr in all this. Anyway, I was at the facility for six months. I was understanding my anger issues, but I still needed therapy. When I got discharged, Ross' dad and mom picked me up and took me home with them. Ross' dad owned a heating and air conditioning company and gave me a job. I enjoyed the work, and he sent me to the local technical college to study the subject."

"I never dropped Dillon off at their house."

"No, I stayed with my mom and dad on the weekends with Dillon."

"Well, thank goodness for that. We already confused the kid as it was."

"I'm very well aware of that, Mary Ann. Is that why you moved to another town because Dillon was so confused?"

"Mark, I had bills to pay. I got a job that paid more than the two jobs I was working combined. It also allowed me more time with Dillon at night. My moving never interfered with your weekends, did it?"

"No, but finding out you had moved from Dillon was strange."

"Oh yeah, like I knew where you were? That's why I had to send the divorce documents to you with Dillon. You know. The documents you never would sign and return."

Mark looks into Mary Ann's angry eyes sorrowfully. "Look, I don't want to fight right now. Let me finish the story, give you my proposition, and then we can fight all you want." Mary Ann huffs out a puff of air and nods. "So I lived with Ross' parents, went to school and therapy, and worked. That's where the money came from that I sent back with Dillon for both of you, which reminds me. What was in the envelope you gave me last night?"

"It is a cashier's check."

"For what?" Mark asks, confused.

"I didn't want or need your guilt money. I used what I needed for Dillon and put the rest in a savings account to either pay for Dillon's college or give back to you. The cashier's check is the money I didn't use, plus interest." Mary Ann looks Mark straight in the eyes as she says the words.

Tears fill Mark's eyes, and he looks down at the table. "That wasn't guilt money. I meant it to help you and Dillon live a good life without me."

Mary Ann stands quickly, almost knocking her chair over. She puts her hands on her hips. "You stupid fool. I didn't want your damn money. I only wanted you and your love. As badly as you hurt me, I would have taken you back. I loved you so much." Tears flow down her cheeks as she runs into the next room. She sits in the living room crying. God, how she loved that man. She would have crawled through hot coals to get him back. She was selfish, though. She didn't want Dillon's father back because she wanted her husband, lover, and best friend back.

Watching Mary Ann run from the room, Mark sits in shock. She would have taken him back. She still loved him even then. He shakes his head and gets up from the table. Instead of following Mary Ann, Mark cleans the kitchen so he can think. He puts the rest of Mary Ann's sandwich in a plastic bag and washes the dishes. Mary Ann enters the kitchen just as Mark finishes.

"Sorry, you can finish your story now," she says, sitting at the table wiping her nose.

"Would you like to return to the living room and be more comfortable?" Mark asks. Mary Ann shakes her head, so Mark sits back down across from her.

"Mary Ann, I couldn't come back. I was still a broken man with things to work out. I still attend therapy sessions, but now, they are once a week instead of three times a week. I could have snapped at any time." Mary Ann glances over at Mark, and he looks down in shame.

"To continue, I finished school and worked. Finally, I moved up in the business and was promoted to sales. Then, I saved up enough to get my apartment and vehicle. I took Dillon to my place on the weekends."

"So you gave us money and didn't have enough for yourself?"

"I guess you could look at it that way, although I didn't. The two of you were my responsibility, and I did it gladly. Being in sales, I had more free time. I could attend Dillon's baseball games and sometimes his practices."

Mary Ann studies Mark for a few seconds and then says, "I never saw you at any games or practices."

"I made sure you didn't. Mom and dad were meeting you halfway to get Dillon. Then my dad died, but mom insisted on still meeting you to pick up Dillon. You didn't attend the funeral, did you?"

"I'm sorry about your dad. No, I didn't. I couldn't face the chance to see you and fall apart all over again."

Mark watches Mary Ann and feels her pain. Although he saw her at Dillon's games and practices, he knew the feelings of shame he felt whenever he saw her.

"Mary Ann, didn't you ever ask Dillon about me?"

"No, I never did. I swore I wouldn't be one of those women who asks about where you lived, what you were doing, did he see you with a woman, and so on. Dillon didn't need or deserve that. All he needed to know was that I loved him. The only thing I ever asked was if he had a good time with his dad. He didn't volunteer any information either." Mary Ann laughs suddenly. "You were the fun parent, and I was the mean old mom."

"Your laugh is still a joy to hear," Mark says with a smile and a warm look in his green eyes. Eyes that could still make Mary Ann melt if she let herself have any feelings. "Dillon got into trouble when I had him."

"Mark, he was a straight-A student and a good kid. So what was there is get into trouble about?"

"Okay, you got me there, but he still acted up sometimes and treated people rudely. I think he tested me to see what he could get away with."

Mary Ann laughs again. "Yes, he was good at testing limits. Please, continue with your story."

Mark nods. "When Mr. Johnson, Ross' dad, got ready to retire, he wanted to give me the business. I refused but said I would buy it from him if I could make payments. After arguing, he finally agreed and had his attorney draw up the papers. There were changes I had always wanted to see happen, but Mr. Johnson was adamant about keeping the business as it was. So, when he retired, I threw myself into making those changes and growing the company. It grew fast and into several states. That's why when Dillon went to college in California, I could move there to monitor him."

"I'm glad you did, so he would have one parent watching out for him. All kinds of things can happen to a young man in college," Mary Ann says as tears form in her eyes.

Mark reaches across the table and takes her hand in his. "What happened with Dillon, Kitten?"

"I don't wish to speak about Dillon right now. Maybe later." She wipes the tears rolling down her cheeks with her free hand. Mark notices she doesn't pull her hand away from his, so he squeezes it.

"Well, that's about it. My company grew, Dillon graduated and came to work for me, and the rest is history, as they say."

"That's not all the story. What happened with Katie?"

"Let's take a break before we go down that road. Come on. Let's get out of here and go for a drive. We can be just two people enjoying the scenery."

"That sounds like a great idea."

Mark stands, still holding her hand, and pulls Mary Ann to her feet. He deliberately pulls harder than is necessary. She ends up almost against him. Mark smells her perfume. It is the same one he always bought for her. Looking into her eyes, Mark sees a spark of something, but just as quickly as it was there, it is gone.

Standing so close to Mark, Mary Ann feels the heat from his body, and it stirs feelings she thought were long dead inside her. His cologne is heady, and she inhales deeply. Mary Ann looks into Mark's eyes and feels them drawing her in like they always did. His masculinity is overpowering.

Mary Ann backs away quickly. "I'll just get my purse and be ready to go."

Chapter 27

"We'll take my car if that's okay," Mark says as Mary Ann locks the door. She nods. "It is hotter in Arizona than normal for this time of year. I thought we might drive up to the mountains."

"That would be great," Mary Ann says as Mark opens the door for her. He leans in closer than necessary as she gets into the car. Mark brushes a lock of hair behind her ear that has fallen in her eyes. Mary Ann peers at Mark and feels the same tug at her soul she felt on their first date. He brushes her cheek, then removes his hand. Mary Ann almost melts from the heat of his touch. Mark closes the door and walks around to his side of the car. This allows Mary Ann to study his chiseled jawline below a perfect profile and his salt and pepper hair.

As Mark gets into the car, he says, "let's not get into any more stories on the drive. They can wait until later."

"I agree. Besides, I want to hear about your company."

Mark starts the car, puts it into reverse, and looks at Mary Ann. "It isn't just my company."

"Oh, okay. You said nothing about a partner."

"I have a silent partner. You." Mary Ann's forehead creases, and her mouth drops open. "Legally, you are still my wife, so half of everything I have is yours."

"But I want nothing," she stammers.

"I know, but I want to ensure you are always taken care of like I always have."

"It's unnecessary. I have savings and a good retirement. I'm financially stable and have money to do what I want."

"Kitten, even if we get a divorce or I die, you will still be taken care of. I have made all the provisions. Now, let's not argue and enjoy the ride." Mark turns away from Mary Ann and backs out of the driveway. "The primary focus of my company is commercial heating and air conditioning. However, I have some residential customers back in our hometown. I won't change that. I've been very fortunate to bid and win projects that have gotten the company's name out in the commercial world. Since we operate in New Mexico, Arizona, Utah, and California, our primary market is air conditioning, or A/C, as we call it. My research and development group is phenomenal. They have developed a solar system to help our customers offset some of the operational expenses. Dillon is heading up our sales division, and customers love him."

Mary Ann listens intently and then asks, "you said Dillon went to work for you right out of college."

"Yes, his mechanical engineering degree was a bonus. He didn't know a thing about heating or A/C and still doesn't, but he can read blueprints. Dillon's a great troubleshooter as well. He's moved up in the company and worked in every department. I planned to promote him to senior vice president, but I don't know now."

"Why?"

"Well, it appears he hasn't treated you like his mother, and I don't like that."

"Mark, his promotion should have nothing to do with me. If he's earned the promotion, give it to him."

"Well, your opinion as my silent partner counts, so I'll do it, but not until you and I talk about him. Then he and I will have a long, overdue talk."

Mary Ann is silent and watches the scenery go by for several minutes as Mark watches her out of the corner of her eye. He sees her reach up to her cheeks several times and assumes she is wiping away tears.

"Kitten, it's getting cooler. Would you want me to put the top down?"

"I didn't realize this was a convertible. I would love that. Mark, why do you continue to call me Kitten sometimes?"

"Well, that was my nickname for you, and you still are and will always be my Kitten," Mark says, looking over at her for her reaction, but receives none.

"I'm very proud of you, Mark. I always knew you could do whatever you set your mind to. You were always so intelligent. But you never gave yourself enough credit."

"Thank you, but speaking of proud. Look at you! Three college degrees, all while working. You moved up from filing in a law firm to the superintendent of a school district. Wow! Now, that's impressive."

"How do you know all that?" Mary Ann studies Mark's profile, astonished.

"I always knew where you were and what you were doing. Well, except when you moved this last time. I lost track of you, but I would have found you, eventually. That's why the checks stopped. I didn't know where to send them."

"I know you didn't keep up with me through Dillon. He hasn't a clue where I've been and what I've been doing," Mary Ann states. Mark can hear a mixture of regret and disappointment in her voice.

"No, not Dillon, and it doesn't matter how I knew. I just did. Are you ready to talk about Dillon now?"

Mary Ann looks out the side window and takes a deep breath. "I guess so. The topic is not going away. I don't know what happened. I really don't. One minute, we were close, and the next, strangers."

Mark looks over and sees Mary Ann clenching her hands in her lap. He moves his hand over and places it on top of hers. She doesn't pull away. "Would you like me to pull over?"

"No, I can talk. Everything was normal until Dillon went off to college. He never came home after that. I wanted to see him when I had time off, but it was always baseball season, practice, or playoffs. I wanted to fly on weekends to see him, but he always had some excuse. At first, we talked twice a week. Then it tapered off. After the second year, he stopped calling me and wouldn't return my calls. I finally just gave up. I haven't seen him since he left for college."

Mark feels Mary Ann's hands tremble and knows she is breaking down. Since they are driving through a town, he pulls into a parking lot. Mark jumps out of the car and runs to her side of the vehicle. He opens her door and gently pulls Mary Ann out of the car just as she sobs. Mark pulls her to him and wraps his arms around her tightly, letting her cry. He thinks it feels incredible to have her in his arms again, even if she is crying. Mary Ann's body molds into his just like it always did.

Mary Ann cries for several minutes in Mark's arms. She pulls her head from his shoulder and looks at him. Mark removes a handkerchief from his back pocket and tenderly wipes the tears from her face. Next, he runs his thumb over her lips, searching her eyes for any sign of feelings for him. He sees her eyes turn dark blue for a few seconds before she looks down.

"Thank you, Mark," Mary Ann says, taking the handkerchief from his hand and backing out of his arms. Then, without another word, she climbs back into the car. Mark closes the door, returns to his side, and drives.

"Mary Ann, I'm so sorry. I did not know. I asked Dillon about you. His response was always that you were doing well. Sometimes he would say that between both of your schedules, the two of you were playing phone tag. Why didn't you attend his graduation or wedding?"

"I wasn't invited to his graduation. I started just to show up, but I knew you would be there for him and celebrate with him. As far as the wedding, I knew nothing about it. Hell, I didn't know he was gay until last night."

"You did not know he was gay?"

"No, Mark. He showed no sign that he was. He dated many girls in high school, as all jocks do. I knew he was sexually active because he never hid his porn magazines or condoms. I never discussed sex with him because that was your job."

"Kitten, does it bother you?"

"What? That he's gay? Of course not. All I ever wanted was for him to be happy and find someone he could love as much as I loved you. What about you?"

Mark takes a few seconds before answering. "I had a feeling he was gay when he got to college. Dillon dated a few girls, but I think that was because he was on the baseball team, so it was expected. Then he threw himself into his studies. I wasn't sure until he injured his knee."

"I didn't know he injured his knee."

"Yeah, he tore it up in a game his senior year. It ended his career. Anyway, while I was in the surgical waiting room, a young man came in, introduced himself as Dillon's friend, and stayed with me. That's when I knew for sure. Dillon has had several serious relationships since college. One lasted almost five years, and then he found Devon. It was love at first sight, Dillon said. They've been together for a long time."

"What was their big news?"

"They have found a surrogate to carry their baby."

"Now, you will be a grandfather."

"You'll be a grandmother, too."

"I doubt that. It's too late."

"It's never too late, Kitten."

"Is Dillon still at your house?"

"No, I was so angry after you left. I told them to leave and go home."

Mary Ann notices the tension around Mark's eyes. "Does he live close by?"

"No, they live in California. I'm sure they got a hotel room and flew out this morning."

"Did he call you?"

"I don't know. I turned my phone off when I got to your house and haven't turned it back on. I didn't want any interruptions while we talked. You were my priority."

"I guess you could turn it on now and see," Mary Ann says.

"No, I'm not ready. Besides, there is something I want to show you, and we're here," Mark replies, pulling into a parking area. "Come on." Mark opens the door for Mary Ann after he gets out.

As she gets out of the car, Mary Ann looks around. "I know this place very well."

"That's good to hear." Mark reaches for her hand and guides her up a hill. "I guess you need different shoes, but I didn't plan to come here. It just happened."

"I'll be okay as long as we take it slow."

Chapter 28

The couple walks for several minutes until they reach a flat area where they stop. Both look around and inhale deep breaths of the fresh air.

"I'm still amazed by how quiet it is here. I come here at least once a month to relax and reflect," Mark says, overlooking the valley below.

"I know. Every year I come here on the same day. I've never missed a year. But I came here again a few weeks ago," Mary Ann states. "This is where you proposed to me." She looks over at Mark.

Still holding her hand, Mark squeezes it. "Do you always come on that day?"

"Always. It was a very special day in my life that I will always treasure."

"Me, too. You said yes, and I was so happy. I couldn't understand why you wanted to marry me. I was just a poor kid with no plan for the future."

"You were always the boy with a terrible reputation with girls and taking risks. I couldn't understand you wanted to marry ME. I was so boring and plain."

"You were beautiful. I fell in love with you the first time I saw you."

Mary Ann laughs and says, "well, it took you long enough to ask me out."

"I was terrified you would say no." Both people stand silent for several minutes, gazing at the mountains in the distance, still holding hands. Then Mark looks down at Mary Ann's hand and says, "you still wear your rings."

"I don't know why you're surprised. We are still married." She looks down at Mark's hand. "I see you still wear yours, too."

He turns to look into Mary Ann's eyes. "I always will, even if we divorce. You are the only woman I ever want to be married to." Mark hesitates for a minute and then says, "are you ready to hear my proposition?"

"Sure," Mary Ann answers, removing her hand from his, taking a step away, and putting a little distance between them.

"Let's sit down." They sit down on a big rock side by side. "I told you my story, and I swear it's the truth. I have loved no one, but you and I never will. My love for you is as strong as it ever was. No, it's stronger. I guess time does that."

Mark pauses for a few seconds. Then he takes a deep breath, looks at Mary Ann, and continues. "My proposition is this. I would like you to be my wife again for thirty days. I will sign the divorce papers at the end of the thirty days, if that's what you want."

Mary Ann stares at him for what seems like an eternity before speaking. "What do you mean by being your wife?"

"I want you to be my wife in every way. I want us to do everything together. We will cook and clean together, travel, and be intimate like we were before."

"You're kidding, right?" Mary Ann stammers.

"No, I'm not. I want us to be close to each other. I want to make love to you at least one more time before I die."

Mary Ann's eyes are big as saucers. "What do you hope to gain by this and be honest with me?"

"I at least want us to be friends again. If more happens, I would be the happiest man on earth. If you still want the divorce, I hope we can at least be friends, but if you want, I will be out of your life forever."

"You're kidding me. Do you want to act like nothing ever happened? I can't believe this. Why now?"

Mark's eyes fill with tears. "Because I am at peace with myself, I don't have to worry about the possibility of physically hurting you. All the years of therapy have helped me to control my demons. I also know full well what I have missed all these years by not being by your side."

"Oh, my God! I can't believe this. Why not just leave things as they are? We can celebrate our 50th wedding anniversary in a few years alone as we have every anniversary since you left?" Mary Ann yells.

Mark studies Mary Ann before answering. "Because we are both getting older. I have deprived you of a lifetime. But, most of all, I've missed you."

"No, you kept me a prisoner for a lifetime. What if I don't agree with your preposterous proposition?"

"Then no divorce, no friendship, no nothing. Things will go on as they have been, and you will never hear from me again. But, Kitten, you loved me once. Perhaps you can again." Mary Ann stands, walks a few feet away, and looks over the mountains. "I don't need an answer now. You can take a few days and think about it. You can take a week if you need it."

She turns and looks hard at Mark for several minutes. Then she turns back to the mountains.

"Mary Ann, say something and be honest with me," Mark pleads.

She turns around. "Okay, Mark. I'll be honest. I don't want to be hurt again. I still haven't fully gotten over when you left and I don't think I ever will."

"That's the good thing about my proposition. This time I won't leave. It will be you that leaves. Look, if it makes you feel any better, I'll put everything in writing that we can sign. As a show of good faith, I'll have a lawyer draw up divorce papers we can agree on ahead of time. That way, if you choose to leave, it will be immediate. As I said, I will make sure you will be taken care of for the rest of your life. Agree to that."

"Mark, I told you I don't want your money or company."

"I know, but it will give me peace of mind."

Mary Ann turns back to look at the mountains. The tension is so thick that Mark feels an enormous weight pressing down on his broad shoulders.

She doesn't turn around. Mary Ann says, "you made a promise to me right in this very spot that you would love me forever, keep me safe, and take care of me."

"Kitten, I didn't break those promises. Again, that's why I left. I needed to keep you safe. I know it's hard to believe. Would you feel better if you talked to my therapist? I'm willing to do whatever it takes to help you decide. We both will have to live with the decision for the rest of our lives."

Mary Ann turns slightly so she can look at Mark over her shoulder. "What about Katie and the kids?"

He pauses and walks over to her. Placing his hands on Mary Ann's shoulders, Mark turns her around to face him. Then, using his index finger, Mark tilts her head up so he can view into her eyes.

"I've done enough talking about the past for today. I don't want to speak about Katie now. But, I will tell you this. Katie and the kids are part of my past. There was never anything between us, and the kids aren't mine. I'm sure of that. You can just ask if you want a DNA test to prove it, and I'll get one."

Mary Ann peers into Mark's eyes and can see the sincerity he is trying to express in his words. She feels the heat from his hands on her shoulders and the warmth inside herself. A warmth she hadn't felt since he left. "Are you serious about the making love comment?"

"Very much, but I will not force you. I want you to want it as much as I do." Mary Ann shivers, and Mark assumes she is getting chilled, so he wraps his arms around her for warmth. "Come on. You're getting cold, and we better think about getting back." His hands move up to Mary Ann's face. He looks at her full lips. He is drawn to her lips and places a soft kiss there before releasing her. Mark then takes one hand and begins guiding Mary Ann down the path back to the car.

About halfway down, Mary Ann stops. Mark turns around. "Are you okay?"

"Mark," Mary Ann says quietly. "What if I need over thirty days?"

"You can have all the time you need. Thirty days is just a starting point as far as I'm concerned." Mary Ann nods, and the couple walks on.

When they reach the car, Mark holds the door open for Mary Ann, gets in himself, and begins driving back to her house. "I thought we might stop for dinner on the way back. Would that be okay?"

"That will be fine as long as we don't talk about us," Mary Ann answers.

Mark reaches over the console and squeezes her hand in agreement. The ride back to the city is quiet. Mark knows he has given Mary Ann a great deal to think about.

When they reach the city, Mark remembers he and Mary Ann ate pizza on their first date. He wonders if she remembers. "Is pizza okay with you?" he asks.

"Pizza sounds wonderful," she answers.

Mark pulls into a family-owned pizza parlor he is familiar with that reminds him of his high school days. Once the couple is inside and seated, they look over the menu.

"Mark, you pick the pizza only please don't get a thick crust. I want the pizza we had when we were kids."

Mark smiles at her. Mary Ann might not say it, but she remembers their pizza dates just by that comment. He also remembers what she likes, so he orders half pepperoni and half beef with extra cheese.

While the couple waits on their pizza, Mark and Mary Ann discuss politics more in-depth and are surprised to learn they share very similar opinions and voting practices. Mark does a wonderful impression of the current president and has Mary Ann in tears with laughter by the time their pizza arrives.

The conversation turns to their parents while they eat. Mark's mother is still alive but living in Alzheimer's care facility. She no longer recognizes Mark, and Mary Ann notices it bothers him a great deal. He was always closer to his mom than his dad.

Both of Mary Ann's parents are gone, which Mark knew. He tells her he attended both of their funerals but stayed at the back of the church so Mary Ann wouldn't see him. However, he tells her he always felt close to them since he and Mary Ann lived with them for a few months after they got married before and after Dillon was born.

After dinner, Mark drives back to Mary Ann's house and walks her to the door. "Kitten, will you think about my proposition, or am I forty years too late?"

"Yes, Mark. I will seriously consider it," she replies.

"Good. Oh, wait. Can I have your phone for a second?" Mary Ann reaches into her purse, pulls out her phone, and hands it to Mark. He presses a few buttons and hands it back to her. "I programmed my phone number in. Text me later, so I have your phone number. You can call or text me with questions or concerns. I'll see my attorney in the morning and start working on the divorce papers."

"Thank you. It's been a very interesting day. I enjoyed the drive to the mountains. Good night." Mary Ann walks into the house, leaving Mark on the doorstep, wishing he had just taken her into his arms and kissed her the way she wanted him to.

Mark walks back to his car, feeling the weight of the day heavy in his heart. He wants Mary Ann to agree to his proposition so badly. Mark knows he can get her to fall in love with him again if she will just give him a chance.

Exhausted from the day, Mary Ann leans against the door until she hears Mark's car start and drives away. Then, moving away from the door, she tosses her purse on the sofa and looks around her living room for a long time, not seeing anything. Her mind is moving like the middle of a NASCAR race, around and around a track with other cars crowding for a better position.

Deciding a shower might make her feel better, Mary Ann strips out of her clothes as she moves toward her bathroom. She turns the shower on and steps inside. Standing under the almost too hot water, Mary Ann lets the cascading water run over her body.

It reminds her of Mark running his hands over her this morning while he talked.

She thinks I never knew he watched me sleep and my body change. Mark said nothing about it. Instead, he always told her she was beautiful and sexy, even during her eighth and ninth months of pregnancy, when she felt like a baby elephant.

Mark never complained about buying ice cream and pickles in the middle of the night. He said nothing about her swollen feet and ankles when he massaged them while in his lap. Mark was perfect. He was the ideal husband and partner until he left.

Mary Ann washes the day off as tears roll down her face. When finished, she dries off and slips into a plain, cotton gown that Mark would never have approved of. Mary Ann makes her way to the bed, left unmade before lunch. She lies down after playing with Lucy for several minutes and closes her eyes, but sleep refuses to come.

Mary Ann lies awake thinking about the dates she and Mark went on. The first time they had sex. The time she is sure she got pregnant. She relives their wedding day and their three years of happy marriage. Mary Ann thinks about the birth of Dillon and how happy Mark was. Then everything began crashing down around her head, and she never knew why. She saw his drinking begin and get heavier. Then Mark was just gone.

Mary Ann knew Ross' death affected Mark a great deal. Mark changed and became distant. All these years, she thought it was her fault, but today he said it wasn't. How could she be sure? Maybe it was her fault. Maybe their marriage wasn't as strong as she thought because, obviously, Mark didn't share his grief with her or his problems.

Mark had been an excellent father to Dillon. Although she didn't tell him, Mary Ann had seen him at some of Dillon's baseball games throughout the years. She had seen him at her parents' funerals. Every time she saw him, Mary Ann felt the unbearable pain all over again. So it had been a relief when Dillon went off to college. She knew Mark moved to California to be close to his son. Mary Ann also knew she wouldn't have to see him, and she healed, or so she thought.

Now, after all these years, Mark was back with his story and wild proposition. How dare he? How dare he indeed? Why couldn't he just leave things as they were? Could she believe him? Could she play the part of a wife for thirty days to get the divorce she deserved? Could she be that close to him without revealing her feelings? Finally, sleep came at 3:00 am.

Chapter 29

Mary Ann wakes at 10:00 am with a splitting headache. She knows it's from all the crying she did yesterday. When she looks in the mirror, Mary Ann is horrified. Her eyes are almost swollen shut, her nose is a bright shade of pink and sore, and her lips are all puffy. "Lucy, it looks like I'm staying home with you today," Mary Ann says to the cat who has jumped on the counter. "I can't go anywhere looking like this."

After dressing and having breakfast, Mary Ann walks out into the bright sunshine to retrieve her newspaper. As she walks back to the house, she hears a faint voice say excuse me. Mary Ann looks around, shocked to find the elderly woman who lives next door to William hobbling toward her.

"Excuse me, miss," the frail woman says.

Mary Ann crosses the street, so the woman doesn't have to walk much further.

"Yes, ma'am. Can I help you?"

"I'm really sorry to bother you, but I know you are friends with William next door. But I haven't seen him in a few days, which is highly unusual. He waters his plants daily, but he hasn't been. So could you check on him? I'm distraught over not seeing him."

"I would be happy to check on him. He gave me a key to his house several months ago. So I'll check on him and let you know how he is," Mary Ann tells the woman. "I'll go right now."

Mary Ann hurries to her house and finds the key she forgot to give back to William when she told him their relationship was over. Mary Ann crosses the street to William's house and unlocks the door. She intends to crack the door and call out to him.

She opens the door to peek in, but the stench is overwhelming. Mary Ann closes the door quickly, turns, and retches into the shrubs next to the front door. At the same time, Mark is pulling into Mary Ann's driveway and sees her. He runs over to her and catches her as she passes out.

When Mary Ann opens her eyes, she is lying in Mark's arms on her bed. She grabs him and begins crying.

"Oh, Mark."

"I know, Kitten, and I'm so sorry."

"I. I need to get up and call someone."

"It's all taken care of. All you need to do is lie here and rest.

"Have I been out long?"

"Long enough for the officials to come and take the gentleman away."

Mary Ann snuggles closer to Mark, thankful to have his muscular arms around her now. The doorbell rings, interrupting the quiet moment.

"I'll get it and be right back," Mark says. He unhooks himself from Mary Ann's grasp and climbs off the bed. He is gone for several minutes and then returns. "That was Greta, wanting to check on you."

"She's a friend and takes care of Lucy when I travel."

"I assume that's Lucy," Mark says, pointing at Mary Ann's back. Lucy has curled against Mary Ann's back, sleeping.

"Yes, that's Lucy," Mary Ann smiles. "Mark, do you know who William is or was?" Mark shakes his head as he lies back beside Mary Ann, pulling her into his arms. "William was Katie's husband she left years ago. He was also the man I was seeing before Katie showed up."

Mark is quiet for a minute and then asks, "was it serious between the two of you?"

"According to him, it was. We stopped seeing each other when the police brought Katie to his house. After she was gone, William came over and told me the story that was in the newspaper. He wanted me to hear it from him before I read it. He wanted to get back together, but I told him no. Oh, no! What if my rejecting him and something to do with his death?"

"Kitten, we may never know, but I can tell you that his death was more likely natural. Greta said the police told her there was no sign he took his own life. But his heart might have given out after all he had been through."

"I hope he didn't suffer. William had been through so much. He was a very nice man. It took a while to get him to lower the wall he built around himself so we could be friends. This is so sad."

Mark hugs Mary Ann and then says, "I know it was hard for you when you opened the door." She nods. "I have an idea. Come stay at my house for a few days and get over the shock of William's death." Mary Ann rises and looks at Mark, confused. "Kitten, this has nothing to do with my proposition. This is about your well-being. You will have your own bedroom, ensuite, and all the privacy you want. You can relax, lie by the pool, or whatever you want."

"That's very sweet of you, Mark, but I have Lucy."

"You can bring Lucy with you. I won't mind. I always liked cats. I just never had one of my own."

"Why are you even here, Mark?"

"Two things. Well, actually three. First, I wanted to check on you. I gave you a lot to think about yesterday, and you were so upset and crying most of the day. Second, I wanted to tell you I met with the attorney about the divorce papers."

"Okay, but you could have just sent me a message. So what's the third thing?"

"Well, the divorce papers will be ready tomorrow. I wanted to ask if you would have dinner with me tomorrow night to go over the agreement."

"Mark, I told you I didn't want any of your money, but I suppose you are stubborn and did whatever you wanted."

"Stubborn? You think I'm stubborn?" Mark reaches over and tickles Mary Ann just like he used to. She giggles and tries to pull away, but he won't get her to go. The sound of her laughter makes his heart beat faster in his chest.

Mark's love for her overtakes him. He leans over, and kisses her. At first, Mary Ann doesn't respond, but then her lips part as if inviting him and Mark takes advantage. The kiss deepens with desire for both of them. Mark pulls Mary Ann on top of him. She runs her fingers through his graying hair while the kissing continues. They kiss for several minutes before Mary Ann pulls away and gets off Mark and the bed. She is panting just as hard as he is.

"I better make us some lunch," she says breathlessly, leaving the room almost running.

Lucy raises her sleepy head and looks at Mark. "Well, at least I know there's still some feeling there. Now, to harness it and make it grow," he tells the cat before getting off the bed himself.

Chapter 30

"Ham and cheese sandwiches okay with you?" Mary Ann asks when Mark walks in. She has her back to him.

"Sure. Can I have two?"

Mary Ann turns and smiles. "Of course. Would you grab the chips? I'm drinking water. Do you want coffee?"

"Yes, to all the above, and I'll make the coffee."

"Okay, make enough for me. I have cake for dessert." The couple move around the kitchen, comfortable with each other.

When they sit down to eat, Mary Ann says, "you probably don't want to talk about Katie, but I'm going to tell you what William told me. You can jump in, but I will not consider your proposition until I hear your side of the story."

"That's fair enough," Mark says.

Mary Ann tells Mark what William told her. When she's finished, she looks at Mark with questioning eyes.

"Okay, here goes. What William told you is all true. What you don't know is this. Katie was Ross' little sister. She was two years younger than you, so you probably didn't know her while you were in school. Katie was a good kid who worshipped Ross. She would follow him around like a puppy. It got on his nerves and mine, but he loved her. He made me promise to look after her if anything should happen to him."

Mark pauses briefly, looks at Mary Ann, and proceeds. "When Ross died, Katie lost her way to where her parents sent her to live with an aunt and uncle for a while. Based on what you told me, I assume she dated William before she left. When she came back home, Katie was pregnant. She got married, I guess, to William then."

"That makes sense," Mary Ann says.

"I lost track of Katie because of everything I was going through. Then in 1991, I was looking to buy a house in Prescott. I walked into a real estate office, and there was Katie. I took her to lunch. We caught up on almost everything. I never talked about you to her. I saw her several times because of my dealings with the real estate agent. Then one day, totally out of the blue, Katie called me and said she was being abused by her husband and had to get away from him."

"You believed her?" Mary Ann asks.

"Well, I did at first. Katie came up with this elaborate plan to get away. She never told me the details of her plan. By that time, I had purchased a house in another city. I picked her up and took her to my house. I didn't mind helping Katie, but she had expensive tastes. That's when I told her she would have to get a job. The next thing I knew, she was pregnant and then pregnant again. That's when I bought a different house with a cottage for her. I didn't want her kids tearing up my place. I was still helping her financially."

"That was very kind of you, Mark," Mary Ann says.

"Well, I had promised Ross." Mark takes a deep breath. "Then here comes another baby. I had just about had my fill of Katie when

I found the stuff she was shoplifting. She lied at first, but then admitted that her job at the bar didn't pay enough for her and the three kids. I knew that was a lie because she was living at my place rent-free, and I bought the food for her and her kids. That's when I kicked her out. I felt bad about it, but I couldn't take it anymore. I don't know where she went."

Mary Ann lays her hand on top of his. "I think you did more than enough for her. She needed to help herself."

"I know, but I still felt guilty. Katie called me the first time she got arrested for shoplifting. I paid her fine and got her out of jail for the kids. Then the next time she called, I wouldn't pay the fine. I didn't hear from her again until she called about the necklace. She said a friend gave her the necklace, but she needed money. She wanted me to take it to a pawnshop. I checked it out and knew she wouldn't get near the amount the necklace was worth. So I gave her $2,000 and told her I would keep it until she wanted it back. You know the rest."

"Mark, there's a story behind that necklace. William gave it to me originally after we started spending more and more time together. He liked Lucy and said he thought of me when he saw it because of her. I gave it back to him when he told me Katie was coming to his house and we shouldn't see each other until he got things straightened out."

Mark studies Mary Ann for several seconds. Then he says, "it sounds like things were getting deep between the two of you."

"No, Mark. I could never have gotten serious with him or anyone else, for that matter. There wasn't room in my heart for another man. Besides, I couldn't have married them, anyway." Mary Ann removes her hand from Mark's and looks down at her plate.

"Kitten, I was serious when I said there was never anything between Katie and me. I will admit to dating a few women, but that was a long time after I left you. There was never any serious relationship or anything close because I only loved you and didn't want anyone else. I hope you believe me."

"I just don't know what to believe right now, Mark. I believe you about Katie and the kids, though."

"It's okay, Kitten. I understand. Now, how about my offer to come to stay at my house?"

"You know, Mark, under the circumstances of this morning, I think I'll take you up on your offer. Are you sure you don't mind Lucy coming along?"

"I'm sure. Why don't I clean up while you go pack for you and Lucy? Will you need your car?"

"No, I don't think so."

"If you do, I'll bring you back to get it."

"Okay, Mark. I'll go pack."

Mark cleans the kitchen and walks into the living room when he hears his name being called. "Mary Ann, do you need me for something?"

"Yes," she replies from the bedroom. "Would you look under the sofa for mice?"

"Mice? What the hell, Mary Ann?"

Mary Ann comes to the doorway laughing. "Yes, mice. Lucy's favorite toys. She hides them under the sofa."

"Oh, good Lord," Mark says, shaking his head. He gets down on all fours, looking under the sofa. Sure enough, there are about a dozen little stuffed mice of various colors. "Does Lucy have a favorite color?" he asks.

Mary Ann sits down on the sofa next to him. "She prefers red or green."

"Well, I don't see red or green," Mark says, looking up at Mary Ann, who has a big smile on her face.

"Mark, I was kidding. Cats are color blind."

"Is that so?" Mark says. He reaches for Mary Ann's bare foot and tickles it. She lies down on the sofa because she is laughing so hard. Her head is inches away from Mark's. He stops tickling her foot and looks at her.

Mary Ann sees pure love and desire in Mark's eyes. It makes her tingle all over, so she reaches out and touches his face. She wishes to kiss him so hard at that moment, but Lucy jumps on the sofa. Thank you, Lucy, Mary Ann thinks to herself.

"I'm almost finished packing," Mary Ann says, rising from the sofa. "Can I have three or four mice?"

It takes Mark two trips to his car to carry a litter box, litter, cat carrier, and a box containing Lucy's food and toys. Then he returns for Mary Ann's one suitcase while she carries Lucy.

Once in the car, Mary Ann holds Lucy in her lap. After Mark gets in and starts the car, he looks over at the two females and says, "I swear, Kitten. We never had to carry this much stuff around for Dillon when he was a baby. You had one diaper bag with everything in it."

Mary Ann laughs and hugs Lucy. "Well, Miss Lucy is a little girl and needs her things."

"You know, maybe you should look into teaching her to use the toilet like those cats I read about on the internet," Mark says, backing out of the driveway.

Chapter 31

As Mark and Mary Ann, who's carrying Lucy, approach his front door, the door opens immediately.

"Mr. Green."

"Hi, Stacy," Mark says. "This is Ms. Green and Lucy. They will stay with us for a few days. Will you ask Robert to get the things out of the car and take them to the blue bedroom, please?"

Stacy looks at Mary Ann with confusion but says, "of course. Hello, Ms. Green."

"Please, call me Mary Ann."

"Okay, Mary Ann. Hi, Lucy. Aren't you a beautiful girl? Can I hold her?" Stacy holds her hands open, and Lucy goes right to her. "Lucy, let's go find Robert. I'm sorry, Mary Ann. Would it be okay to take her with me?"

Mary Ann laughs. "Don't ask me. Ask her." Lucy is already purring. Stacy smiles and walks away carrying the cat.

"Come, Kitten. I'll show you your room." Mark reaches for Mary Ann's hand and guides her through the living room.

"Mark, I didn't know you had people."

"Did you think I could take care of this by myself?" he asks, waving across the house.

"I didn't pay any attention to the size of this place the other night."

"Stacy takes care of the house and cooking. Robert is her husband and sees after the grounds and other maintenance issues." Mark and Mary Ann walk into a massive bedroom down the hall from the living room.

"This will be your room for as long as you want to stay," Mark says. The bedroom is almost the size of Mary Ann's entire house. "The ensuite is through that door, and the closet is over there." Marks points to doors as he talks.

"Wow! This is gorgeous," Mary Ann gazes at the room.

"Now, let me show you around." Mark leads the way down the hallway and shows her two more bedrooms. They return to the living room and go through a dining room and kitchen. "Back here is my bedroom and office," Mark says, leading Mary Ann down another hallway.

When they reach his bedroom doorway, Mark turns to her and says, "if you agree to my proposition, this will be your bedroom, too. I hope you say yes, Kitten," he says as he turns and looks into her eyes. Mary Ann blushes under his fiery gaze. "Now, come on." Mark guides her back to the living room and out onto the patio. "Here is the pool. There's a hot tub on the left."

Mary Ann takes a serious breath. "Mark, I'm overcome with happiness for you. You have done well. I'm so proud of you."

"I have been very fortunate," Mark says humbly.

"I know better. You threw yourself into your work and worked hard to make your vision come to life."

Mark turns to Mary Ann and takes a step closer. He releases her hand and touches her face with a gentle caress. "The cost of losing you was more than I could take. I had to keep my sanity," he whispers. Mary Ann leans into his touch for a moment and then backs away, walking to the pool's edge.

"Excuse me, Mr. Green," Stacy appears at the door. "Robert has everything inside. Are you ready for the car to be parked in the garage?" Mark nods, not taking his eyes off Mary Ann. "Mary Ann, Miss Lucy is situated with toys and litter box in the ensuite. I closed the bedroom door so that she couldn't explore. She is so precious."

Mary Ann turns and looks at Mark. "Thank you, Stacy. However, I must warn you that Lucy can be a pest. She will wear you out, wanting you to play with her."

"That's okay. It will be nice to have her here. You, too, of course." Stacy turns and leaves the couple alone.

"Kitten, did you bring a swimsuit?" Mary Ann nods. "Well, let's change, get into the pool, and cool off." Mark follows her into the house. When Mary Ann turns left, Mark turns right.

Mary Ann opens her suitcase and finds her bikini. When packing, she chose one that wasn't too skimpy. Mary Ann changes, grabs her coverup, and slips it on. Then she heads to the pool where she's surprised to find Mark already in the pool. Mary Ann stands inside the door, watching the handsome man as he swims. His forearms are very muscular and tan. His salt and pepper hair shines in the sunlight. It feels like her heart skips a beat with every stroke Mark takes.

As if he senses her presence, Mark climbs out of the pool when he reaches the edge.

"Come swim with me," he says, reaching for a towel.

"Mark, I never learned how, but I'll stay in the shallow end while you swim."

"Okay, Kitten. I just want you to relax and be comfortable here. Let's try the hot tub instead," Mark suggests. He slowly ambles over to her and then touches the flimsy coverup. "You need to get out of this first," he says seductively. "Let me help you." He reaches for the hem of the coverup and pulls it over Mary Ann's head as she raises her arms.

Mary Ann feels naked as Mark's eyes rake over her body from top to bottom and back up.

"You are so beautiful," he says in a reverent tone. "I remember the first time I ever saw you naked. I was afraid to touch you because you might break."

Mary Ann looks at Mark, trying to think of something witty to say, but her brain fails. So she does what her body tells her to. She admires Mark's body, and a long-forgotten yearning takes her when she does. A warmth spreads over her, heading straight to her groin area.

Mary Ann feels the tug of those green eyes. She looks at Mark and spies the fire she saw the first time they made love. The fire seems to pull her into the throes of passion that she wants so badly, but is afraid to trust. Mary Ann looks away and walks over to the hot tub. Mark follows her. He gets into the hot tub, but not before Mary Ann notices a bulge that Mark didn't attempt to hide from her.

Mark lifts his hand to assist Mary Ann into the hot tub. The flame in his eyes is now in his hand. The heat is so intense that Mary Ann feels it almost scorch her skin. She removes her hand from his and sits down.

"Mark, where do Stacy and her husband live?"

Mark clears his throat and answers in a husky voice. "See those trees over there?" he points to the right. "They have a three-bedroom house on the other side. They have room for their kids and grandkids when they visit."

It's almost as if Stacy heard her name because she appears seconds later. "Mr. Green, I brought some lemonade. There's a chicken Caesar salad in the fridge and French Onion soup in the crock pot for dinner. There's also a loaf of French bread in the warmer. Will you need anything else?"

"No, thanks, Stacy. Have a good evening," Mark says.

"Thank you. Mary Ann, would it be okay to play with Lucy a little while before I go home?"

"Of course. Lucy will be ready to play."

"Great, I'll see you both tomorrow at breakfast." Stacy turns and leaves the patio quickly.

"Kitten, I hope soup and salad are okay for dinner."

"That sounds perfect, Mark. Now, I would like to try that lemonade. Can I bring you a glass?"

"I would like that. Thanks."

Mary Ann gets out of the tub and walks several steps to the table. She is aware Mark is watching her every move. Mary Ann pours two glasses of lemonade and turns around.

"Do you like what you see?" she asks shyly, looking into Mark's eyes.

"Very, very much," he answers. His eyes grow darker, and Mary Ann remembers that look.

"You look like you've stayed fit all these years, Mark."

"I have a gym next to my bedroom. I try to work out every day. It helps with stress, and I do a lot of thinking and planning there."

Mary Ann hands Mark his glass. Holding hers, she carefully climbs back into the hot tub. Mary Ann asks questions about the house and grounds. Mark tells her he has lived in the house for ten years. The house is too large for him, but he fell in love with the pool and grounds.

"I never have guests. Dillon and Devon are the only ones that have ever stayed here, and now you."

"Do Dillon and Devon come often?"

"About once a month to visit. Dillon comes every couple of weeks for meetings since the company's headquarters are in Phoenix. Would you like to see him? He should be here next week."

"No, thank you," Mary Ann replies. "I have nothing to say to him."

"You'll have to talk to him, eventually."

"No, I don't. Dillon left me. I didn't leave him. Just like you left me. Must be a pattern for the Green men."

Mark looks at Mary Ann. He sees sadness in her eyes. Then he gets out of the hot tub and jumps into the pool, where he swims several laps. When he gets out, Mark grabs his towel and declares it is almost dinner time and they should change for dinner. He walks into the house, leaving Mary Ann alone.

She lies back in the hot tub and closes her eyes—memories of happier times when Dillon was born, and attentive Mark flooded her mind. Mary Ann smiles, remembering Mark's first attempt at changing a dirty diaper. Next, she thinks about the first time Mark changed Dillon's diaper, and Dillon peed, spraying his dad and himself. Mark was shocked, but Mary Ann fell to the floor, laughing hard. It took both her and Mark to clean up the mess. Then Mark had to shower and change for work.

"You're smiling," a voice whispers in her ear. Mary Ann opens her closed eyes to see Mark kneeling beside her. "What are you thinking about?" Mark's breath tickles her ear and makes Mary Ann tingle all over.

"I was remembering the first time you were changing Dillon and he peed all over you and everything else. Your expression was priceless."

"You thought that was extremely funny and fell on the floor laughing."

Mary Ann giggles. "It had happened to me several times, so I knew eventually you would be on the receiving end."

"I think the two of you planned the timing. I was late for work because we had to clean everything and I had to shower and change. But my boss didn't get mad at me for being late because he was laughing just as hard as you did." Mark's fingertips graze across Mary Ann's face. "You were an exceptional mother."

"You were a great father, Mark. I hope Dillon will be just like you in that regard." Mary Ann looks at Mark. He leans over, places a soft kiss on her lips, and then looks at her. Mary Ann can feel his hot breath on her face. She wants to kiss him so badly, so passionately, but she refuses to give in this time. Instead, Mary Ann says, "I better change." She slides away from Mark and climbs out of the tub.

Mark watches her and then says, "Kitten, you don't have to change if you don't want to. I just slipped on shorts and a t-shirt because I plan to get into the pool again after eating. So your cover-up should be fine."

"No, I think I'll change. I don't want to get chilled inside." Mary Ann wraps the cover-up around her and hurries into the house.

She changes into a sundress, pets a sleeping Lucy, and then heads to the kitchen for dinner. Mark has set everything out on the island for them.

"I enjoy eating here. I can look out. Sometimes, deer wander into the yard," Mark says.

"Do they come into the yard because you put corn out for them?" Mary Ann asks with a smirk.

"I plead the fifth amendment on that. Please, sit down and eat. Stacy is a marvelous cook."

While eating, Mary Ann learns Stacy and her husband have been with Mark since he bought the house. Both do excellent work. Stacy has had a few health issues that almost led to her and her husband leaving. But Mark hired additional help so Stacy could focus on getting better.

After dinner, Mary Ann returns to her room and gets a book she brought. Then she sits on the patio and pretends to read while Mark swims. I don't think there is one ounce of fat on his body, Mary Ann thinks. The dark hair on Mark's chest is now sprinkled with gray, as is his happy trail below his slim waist. His trunks sit low on his hips, just like the boxer underwear Mark always wore. But, boy, she loved it when Mark pulled those boxers down and made love to her.

"You're blushing," Mark says, looking down at Mary Ann.

"Am I? I think it is just the sun setting that makes me look that way. Oh, while I'm thinking about it, what time is breakfast?"

"It is whenever you get up. I have to go to work tomorrow and will be gone all day. So I want you just to relax and hang around here. Stacy or Robert can take you if you need to get your car."

"Okay. I think I'll turn in. It's been a long day full of surprises."

"I hope you sleep well," Mark says as Mary Ann gets out of her chair.'

"I hope you do, too, Mark," she says as she goes inside.

Mary Ann takes a quick shower, plays with Lucy, and climbs into bed. Yes, the day was full of surprises. Some were good, and some were horrible. She thinks about William. Tears form in her eyes. The poor man had a tough life. But, at least, he is at peace now.

Mary Ann lies on her side with Lucy curled at her back. A knock at the door breaks the silence of the room. Knowing it is Mark, she tells him to come in.

"Kitten, I'm sorry to disturb you, but I need to ask you a question," Mark says, walking in and sitting on the bed beside her.

"Couldn't it wait until tomorrow? I'm exhausted."

"No, because it is important to me, and I need to know the answer."

"Okay, Mark. What is your question?"

"Kitten," Mark begins, "sometimes we seem close, and then you pull away. Are you scared of me?" He looks into her eyes as if searching her soul for an answer.

Mary Ann looks down and sits up, using those few seconds to decide her answer. Finally, she looks up at Mark and cups his cheek. "Yes, but not physically. I don't believe you would ever hurt me that way. Not back then and not now. I'm terrified you will hurt me again if I let myself get close to you. I never recovered from the pain and hurt. It is still there inside my heart."

Mark sees the pain in her eyes, and it breaks his heart.

"Mark, Dillon is the only thing that saved me after you left. Sometimes, when he was gone on the weekends, I was so tempted to end it all. I knew you would take care of Dillon if I wasn't around. So I bought pills, razor blades, and even a gun, but I couldn't do it. Even though I wasn't good enough to be the wife you wanted me to be, I knew I had to be a good mother to Dillon."

As tears run down her face, Mark takes her into his arms. "I'm so sorry, baby. I never thought about the hell you were going through. I just thought about how better off you were without me."

Mary Ann moves out of his arms and looks at Mark through her tears. "Does that answer your question?" she asks.

"Yes, Kitten. It does. I need to earn your trust. By doing that, perhaps I can earn your friendship if nothing else." Mark stands and leaves the room. He closes the door behind him.

Then Mary Ann hears a gut-wrenching sob coming from the hallway. She lies down and sobs herself.

Chapter 32

The following morning, Mary Ann wakes, and Lucy isn't on the bed. Mary Ann jumps up and checks the ensuite, but still no Lucy. Mary Ann calls her, but there is no answer, so she checks under the bed. Again, Lucy is nowhere to be found.

Mary Ann rushes out the door, calling Lucy as she goes. When she gets to the kitchen, Mary Ann hears a loud meow. Lucy is lying in Stacy's lap, getting her belly rubbed.

"Lucy, you scared me!"

"I'm sorry, Mary Ann. I heard her scratching at the door, and I let her out. I've closed all the doors so that she will stay in the kitchen and living room area. I have also fed her," Stacy says.

"That's fine. I was just worried since this is an unfamiliar place. I warned you, Lucy can be a pest."

Stacy laughs. "I love it. I have two of my own. I miss them seeing them during the day. Would you like some breakfast?"

Mary Ann looks over at the clock on the microwave. "No, thanks. I can't believe I slept so late." The clock says 10:30.

"Mr. Green said not to bother you, but he has called twice to check on you. You look like you had a rough night. Mr. Green didn't look much better this morning. He skipped breakfast, too."

Mary Ann walks past Stacy and pours a cup of coffee.

"Mary Ann, I'm not trying to be nosy, but Robert and I have been with Mr. Green for a long time. I feel very protective of him."

"I understand, Stacy, and it's okay."

"You're the first woman he's ever brought into the house."

"Katie didn't come here?" Mary Ann asks.

"I don't know who Katie is, but if she ever came to see Mr. Green, I'm sure he met her at his office, not here."

Stacy observes Mary Ann drink the coffee before speaking again. "Mary Ann, I know who you are, or I have an idea."

"Why do you say that? What has Mark said about me?"

"Mr. Green has never spoken about you, but he didn't have to." Stacy pauses as she chooses her next words. "Did Mr. Green show you his office and bedroom?"

"He did, but from the doorway," Mary Ann answers.

"Please, come with me. Lucy, you stay here and be a good girl." Stacy leads Mary Ann to Mark's office first. When Stacy opens the door, Mary Ann walks in, looking around. She walks over to Mark's desk. There are two pictures on the desk. One is of Dillon and Devon. The other is her and Mark's wedding picture. Mary Ann picks up the picture and runs her finger over the glass.

"Now, the bedroom," Stacy says. Mary Ann sets the picture down and follows Stacy to Mark's bedroom. "I'll leave you alone."

Mary Ann watches Stacy close the door behind her. She walks further into the room. Looking to her right, she sees doors that probably go to his closet and ensuite. When she looks to her left, Mary Ann is amazed. Almost the entire wall is pictures of her.

Mary Ann steps closer to inspect the pictures. They are practically in chronological order. First, there's Mary Ann when she and Mark first started dating. Next is their wedding day, followed by different times in her pregnancy. Then, there are pictures of Mary Ann and baby Dillon.

But, it's the next pictures that take her breath away. The pictures are of Mary Ann at Dillon's baseball games, her graduation pictures for all three degrees, and pictures of her when she visited the place Mark proposed every year. There are pictures of Mary Ann at her various apartments, schools, and offices. There is a newspaper clipping when she was named superintendent of the school district and when she retired. The wall covers the last forty years of Mary Ann's life.

Flabbergasted, Mary Ann sits on the floor and stares at the pictures. Mark said he always knew where she was. It's almost as if he was stalking her, Mary Ann thinks.

Stacy knocks on the door softly. "Mary Ann, are you okay?" Stacy asks as she opens the door.

"I can't believe this," Mary Ann declares.

"Mr. Green is an excellent photographer, don't you think?"

"Mark took all these?"

"He said he did, all but the newspaper clippings, of course. He said he had to be out of town those particular days and didn't have advanced notice so he could change his plans."

Mary Ann looks at Stacy and then back to the wall. "I don't know what to think or say about this."

"Please, don't tell him I showed you the wall. I don't want to make him upset. I'm sure he will show you himself when he gets ready."

"Don't worry, Stacy. I won't say anything."

"Mr. Green called to ask about you. I lied and said you were in the shower."

Mary Ann laughs. "Well, I guess I should dress. It has to be lunchtime by now."

"It is, Mary Ann. May I suggest perhaps putting on your swimsuit? The pool area might be a good place to think after eating."

"That's a great idea, Stacy. Thank you." Mary Ann takes one more hard look at the wall of pictures and leaves the suite, closing the door behind her.

Mary Ann does what Stacy suggested. She put on a swimsuit, got her book, ate, and headed for the pool. But first, Mary Ann took her phone into Mark's room and took pictures of the wall. Then she spent all afternoon poolside thinking about Mark, the photos, and his proposition. Mary Ann didn't open her book at all.

When she heard the patio door open, Mary Ann expected to see Stacy, but instead, Mark walks out onto the patio.

"Oh, my goodness!" Mary Ann exclaimed, looking at Mark. He is dressed in a navy suit tailored to fit his body. She can tell immediately that the suit is very expensive. Mark's shirt is light blue, and his tie is blue with specks of green that match his eyes.

"What?" Mark asks as he removes his jacket.

Mary Ann takes a deep breath at the sight of his muscular forearms beneath his short-sleeved shirt. A surge of electricity courses through her body like lightning, settling in her abdomen.

"You look like you just came from a model's photoshoot. You are, you are, well, I can't find the words right now," Mary Ann says, feeling light-headed.

Mark gives her his 1,000-watt smile and bows. "Why, thank you, madam." He lays his jacket on a chair, unties the tie, and unbuttons the top three buttons of his shirt. Mary Ann sees the hair on his chest peeking through the shirt's gap. It takes her breath away.

"How was your day?" Mark asks, sitting next to her on the chaise. Mary Ann has to move over slightly to give him room, thankful she had to look down to do it. Mark would have seen pure lust in her eyes.

"My day was quiet. How was yours?" she says shyly, hoping Mark doesn't see the drops of sweat that have formed on her top lip.

"I had meetings all day long. So that's why I'm dressed like this. I can assure you I don't wear a suit daily to the office." Mark reaches up, wipes the sweat off her top lip, and smiles as Mary Ann blushes.

"Were your meetings productive?"

"Very. I like your bikini, by the way. It is more revealing than the one you wore last night." Mary Ann looks up at Mark, and he gives her a devilish grin.

Mary Ann quickly looks down at her stomach. "Unfortunately, it's so low, it shows my stretch marks."

Mark glides his fingertips over her stretch marks. Then he does something that catches Mary Ann off guard. Mark leans over and plants tiny kisses and nips across her stretch marks. Mary Ann shivers as the sensation runs from her stomach to between her legs.

Unfazed by Mary Ann's shivers, Mark continues the tiny kisses up Mary Ann's stomach. He doesn't stop at her bikini top, where it meets her cleavage. He continues his assault up her chest and neck, stopping at her earlobe, where he gently bites it.

Mary Ann is panting, shaking, and sweating when she opens her eyes to look at Mark.

"Why, Kitten, I do believe you just had an orgasm." Mark flashes Mary Ann his 1,000-watt smile, stands, and walks into the house, grabbing his jacket on the way. Before he closes the door, Mark says, "I brought the divorce papers with me so we can discuss them tonight. Dinner in forty-five minutes if you're up to it."

Mary Ann lies on the chaise, trying to catch her breath. Mark was right. She did orgasm, and she hadn't had one like that since Mark. It shook her to her core. "Dammit," Mary Ann says aloud. He knows just what buttons to push and then ends with the comment about the divorce papers. Mary Ann rolls her eyes but continues to lie there. She waits for her heart to slow down and gain enough strength in her legs to go shower and dress for dinner.

Chapter 33

When Mary Ann comes into the kitchen, no one is around. Then she sees Mark out on the patio at the grill. When she steps outside, Mark acts as if nothing happened.

"Hi, Kitten. I thought we would have steaks tonight. The potatoes are in the oven, and the salad is in the fridge. I hope that's okay with you."

"Sounds delicious," Mary Ann says, walking next to Mark and inhaling the aroma of grilled steak. "Are you ready for me to get everything together?"

"Yes, I believe so. These should be ready in about ten minutes."

Mary Ann turns, going back into the kitchen. She finds everything they need for the potatoes and salad in the fridge. She finds the plates and utensils and sets their places. Mary Ann finishes up as Mark brings the steaks inside.

While they eat, she asks about Mark's meetings. He tells her he won two bids for A/C work in Phoenix. Dillon had been working on the bids for several months. Mark is excited because he hasn't been very successful in the Phoenix market. Mary Ann asks many questions, which please Mark. Although she is a silent partner, the bids affect her even if she doesn't realize it yet.

Together, the couple cleans up the kitchen. Suddenly, Mary Ann's phone rings in the bedroom. She rushes to answer it. When Mary Ann returns to the kitchen, Mark notices she is a little pale.

"Everything alright, Kitten?"

"The call was from William's phone, which surprised me. It was William's son. They are having a private service for William in two days and would like me to attend."

"Well, that's nice of them to invite you. Do you know his kids?"

"No, I never met them, but William talked much about them. He was very proud of them considering what they went gone through."

"Would you like me to go with you?"

"I don't think so, Mark. I will have to ask Stacy or Robert to take me to my house tomorrow so I can get clothes and my car."

"I'll take you because I'm taking the day off tomorrow to spend it with you."

Mary Ann looks at him. "You don't have to keep me company."

Mark turns to her and adds, "But I want to. We'll find something fun to do."

"Okay. I could use a little fun."

"Great. I think you'll enjoy what I have planned. I thought we could get your car on the way back tomorrow evening." Mary Ann nods in agreement. "Now, shall we discuss the divorce agreement?" She rolls her eyes at Mark. "I'll take that as a yes. I'll be right back."

When Mark returns, he has his swim trunks on. He lays the agreement on the island. "I'm going to give you some privacy." He heads toward the patio door while Mary Ann watches. The ripples of muscles across his back almost sends her heart into overdrive. The trunks are tight across Mark's still cute butt. A heated sensation stirs inside Mary Ann. She shakes her thoughts from her head so she can focus on the agreement.

When she finishes reading, Mary Ann takes the agreement in hand and goes out to the pool. She watches as Mark swims, unaware that she is there. He notices her and climbs out of the pool as she stares at the handsome man she has been married to for a long time.

Mark sits down in a chair next to Mary Ann. "I assume you have finished reading. I'm ready to hear your thoughts."

Mary Ann looks at him and takes a deep breath. "Mark, this agreement is too generous. I have no desire to own one-half of your business. The monthly stipend is enormous. I have plenty of my own money. There's no way I could ever agree to this."

"Kitten, as my wife, you are entitled to your share of my business. I already told you that. So you don't have to do anything. You will just get a share of the profits at the end of each quarter as I do. I won't give on that."

Mary Ann shakes her head. "Then, no monthly stipend."

"I won't agree to that either. I will take care of you like I always did. It's up to you whether or not you spend the money."

"Mark," Mary Ann looks down at her lap. "I never wanted your money. I only wanted you," she whispers.

Mark hears her voice quiver. "I know that now, and you know why I left." He reaches over and covers her hand with his. "I'll reduce the monthly stipend if you will take the cashier's check back."

"No, that's your money! I won't take it back."

"Well, what if I put it into an account for your medical expenses?"

"I have excellent medical coverage from my retirement."

"I know, but you'll be on Medicare in a few years, and your insurance will be secondary. As a result, you may incur out-of-pocket expenses. This account would help cover those."

Mary Ann stands and walks over to the side of the pool. "Whatever," she says without looking at Mark. Then she turns to face him. "I will not win this argument, will I?"

"No, Kitten. You won't. I'll reduce the monthly stipend by $1,000, but that's all. I call the attorney and have him make the changes."

Mary Ann turns and looks back at the pool. "Forty-three years of marriage, and it all comes down to money. How stinking sad is that?"

Mark walks behind her and puts his hands on her shoulders. "We're not divorced yet," he whispers in her ear, sending chills down Mary Ann's spine. Mark then turns her around and lifts her chin so he can look into her eyes. "We should turn in. I'll wake you early in the morning for our fun day."

"Okay, Mark. Good night." Mary Ann backs up and walks away.

Chapter 34

True to his word, Mark wakes Mary Ann at 5:00 am. They dress and stop at a fast food place for coffee and breakfast sandwiches before Mark points the car in a westerly direction.

The drive is pleasant because the couple talks about anything but themselves and their son. Three hours later, they arrive at the Grand Canyon National Park. Mark pulls into a parking lot. After opening Mary Ann's door, he takes her hand and leads her to a nondescript building. Once inside, Mark leaves Mary Ann to go to a counter to talk to a gentleman for a few minutes.

Finally, Mark holds out his hand to Mary Ann and says, "let's go." She hurries over to him, and they go out a door at the rear of the building. Outside is a helicopter, ready and waiting.

"Oh, no! I've never been on a helicopter!" Mary Ann yells over the noise.

"Come on, Kitten. I'll be right beside you all the way." Mark squeezes her hand, and she giggles. Then, they climb into the helicopter and start their personal tour of the Grand Canyon. Mark holds Mary Ann's hand during the one-hour tour.

After landing, they exit the helicopter and go back inside the building. The couple uses the restroom and immediately heads back outside, where Mark has arranged an off-road SUV tour. Mark helps Mary Ann climb into the back of the vehicle and then excuses himself for several minutes. When he returns, Mark is carrying a blanket and a large cooler.

The tour guide travels down into the canyon, providing details and history along the way. Then, when the SUV reaches the bottom of the canyon, the tour guide parks near the river.

Mark helps Mary Ann out of the vehicle and then hands her the blanket. He grabs the cooler and leads the way to the river bank a short distance from the SUV.

"Spread the blanket out here," Mark points to a spot near the riverbank. Mary Ann does, and Mark sits the cooler down next to the blanket. He sits on the blanket and pulls Mary Ann down beside him.

"What's in the cooler?" she asks.

"Lunch." Mark opens the cooler and takes out an assortment of cheeses, crackers, and fruits. Next, he takes out plates, napkins, and bottles of water.

"Oh my, Mark. This is wonderful," Mary Ann says as she smiles at him. "Thank you."

"My pleasure. Have you ever been inside the canyon to the river?"

"No. We toured the canyon once when I was a kid, but that's it. Have you?"

"One summer, Dillon and I hiked down here. We camped close to here for two days. We swam, fished, and just talked."

"Mark, I'm so glad you did things like that with Dillon. He needed to be with you. He needed a man in his life after being with his mean mom all the time."

"You weren't a mean mom at all. Dillon worshipped you. He said many times he was lucky to have you for a mom. Although he said he wished you didn't have to work so hard. That reminds me. Dillon is coming in for a meeting the day after tomorrow. I told him to plan on staying over a day. It's time I talk to him."

"Mark, please don't discuss me with Dillon," Mary Ann says in a serious voice.

"I will not talk about that per se, but it is time for him to hear the truth about why I left. So I won't discuss our private life, Mary Ann. I promise."

"Okay, let's just enjoy our lunch and the rest of the day," Mary Ann says with a wistful smile.

After lunch, the couple walks along the riverbank and splashes each other with water before packing up and heading back to the SUV and Phoenix. They stop for burgers on the drive back.

The couple reaches Mary Ann's house at 8:00. As Mark pulls into the driveway and parks, Mary Ann looks over at him and says," it wasn't fair what you did to me yesterday."

Mark looks over at her but doesn't smile. "I know it wasn't, but I had to know if there was any spark there. I think, if you're honest with yourself, you would admit that you needed to know, too."

"Mark, I'm, coming home after the funeral tomorrow." Mark turns his head and looks out the windshield. Mary Ann can see his jaw clench, and he's biting the inside of his cheek. "I need to think about your proposition, and I can't do that at your house."

"Have you thought about it all?" Mark's voice sounds harsh.

"Honestly, not much. The last two days have been crazy." Mark doesn't look at her or say anything. Mary Ann senses his disappointment. "Mark, could I have a couple of extra days? I promise to give you an answer by this time next week."

"Sure, Kitten. You could have a week, I said. I understand." Mark still won't look her way. "I won't bother you. You can call or message me when you're ready."

"Thank you, Mark. Now, I'll get my stuff. It won't take me but a few minutes." Mary Ann gets out of the car and walks to the door. She hears Mark back out of the driveway. Wow! Mary Ann thinks he must be angry because I expected him to follow me back to his house. Oh well. She goes inside, gets her things, and returns to Mark's house.

The house is quiet when Mary Ann walks into his house, so she is silent. Mark is lying on the sofa asleep, with Lucy sleeping in the middle of his chest. Mary Ann smiles and sits down in a chair opposite the couch. She remembers Mark taking naps on the sofa with baby Dillon asleep on his chest.

About half an hour passes before Lucy yawns and stretches. Mark wakes up and sees Mary Ann watching them.

"Have you been watching us long?" he asks.

"Long enough," Mary Ann replies.

"What were you thinking?"

"I remember you asleep on the sofa with Dillon sleeping on your chest like Lucy." Mary Ann smiles at Mark with love in her eyes and then glances away.

"I don't think I ever went fully under. I was subconsciously afraid I would buck Dillon off."

"No, you wouldn't have. You always had a protective arm over him." Mary Ann stands. "I better feed Lucy and go to bed."

"Stacy left a note and said she fed Lucy, but I think you get play time," Mark says as Lucy jumps down and runs to Mary Ann.

She reaches for her things. "Come on, Lucy. Let's try to wear you out so you'll sleep all night. Good night, Mark. Thank you for letting us stay here."

Mark stands and walks over to Mary Ann, almost touching her. She takes a deep breath, inhaling his masculine scent, making her heart race.

"I enjoy having you here. It was nice knowing you were here when I got home." Mark reaches up and caresses Mary Ann's cheek, then drops his hand and walks toward his bedroom.

Chapter 35

Mary Ann plays with Lucy until the cat gets sleepy and lies down. Mary Ann, however, isn't ready for bed, even though it was a long day. Well, I committed to giving Mark an answer in a week, which will require some earnest thinking, she decides. I can't do that here. There's only one place I can go.

She checks to see if the cabin in Eureka Springs is available for a few days. Fortunately, it is, so she books it. Next, she makes flight and rental car arrangements for Little Rock tomorrow afternoon after the funeral. Mary Ann decides to ask Stacy to keep Lucy instead of bothering Greta. With everything in place, she lies down and falls asleep.

Mary Ann is up early the following day, packing her things. She waits for Mark to leave before leaving her room and asking Stacy to keep Lucy. Stacy is thrilled to do so. Mary Ann goes to her house and packs her suitcase before going to the funeral.

The funeral is nice, and she meets William's three kids. A glitch in the funeral occurs when Katie shows up, escorted by two police officers. The funeral director informs Katie she is not welcome, and the three leave.

Mary Ann heads straight to the airport and boards her plane. Once in Little Rock, she picks up the rental car, food, and several bottles of wine before heading to the cabin. It thrills Mary Ann to see the cooler weather so she can spend hours on the deck.

Mary Ann stays four full days and nights at the cabin without leaving except to buy more wine. She cries and curses. Mary Ann remembers the good times and the bad. She has pleasant dreams and nightmares. Then she thinks about her life and her future. Her future is just as her life has been since Dillon left. Mary Ann knows she will never love another man with or without a divorce. She will be alone and fill her time with travel and Lucy to compensate for the loneliness. Mary Ann finally reaches a decision and flies home.

Knowing Mark will be at work, Mary Ann picks Lucy up on her way home from the airport. It is early evening, so she decides to send Mark a message in the morning. Mary Ann falls into a restful, dreamless sleep.

The following morning after breakfast, Mary Ann sends Mark a message.

"I have made my decision. I'm ready to talk."

"Today?" Mark responds.

"If you like."

"This afternoon. My place or yours?"

Mary Ann ponders for several minutes before responding. "The outlook. 2:00."

"I'll be there," Mark messages back.

Now Mary Ann has to develop her plan. She sits down and discusses it with Lucy. Lucy agrees by meowing loudly and then wants to play. They play for a while, and then Lucy heads off to the bedroom for a nap. Mary Ann dresses in jeans, a blouse, and sneakers and leaves for the outlook.

She arrives at the overlook first. Mary Ann is standing looking at the mountains when Mark arrives. Even though he is quiet, Mary Ann smells his cologne and knows he's there. So she turns around, and the sight of Mark takes her breath away.

He's gotten a haircut while she was gone, and he looks a little grayer around his temples. Mark's green t-shirt is tight across his chest, displaying his muscles under the shirt and his bare forearms. It also makes his eyes greener. His black jeans fit snugly, accenting his slender waist and hang on his hips. Mary Ann licks her lips as her heart pounds in her chest.

"Hi, Mark. Thanks for meeting me here."

"Sure, Kitten. It's nice to see you."

"You too, Mark. Please sit down." Mary Ann points to the large, familiar rock. She watches as he does and sees a sprinkling of his chest hair peeking out from the t-shirt collar. She shakes her head to clear her mind.

Once Mark is seated, Mary Ann goes over to him and kneels between his legs.

"I'm ready to hear your answer," Mark whispers, looking down at her.

"Okay. Here goes," she says, taking his hands. "Mark, you and I both know we can never go back to the way things were. Too many years have passed. We are also not the same people we were back then. We really don't know each other. It would be extremely hard for me to crawl into bed with a man I hardly know."

Sensing what Mary Ann is about to say, tears slide down Mark's face as he lowers his head. She reaches up and wipes his tears.

"Mark, look at me. Please." He looks up and looks directly into Mary Ann's eyes. "I've given this much thought, and I have a counter proposition for you."

"A counter proposition?" Mark whispers.

"Yes." Mary Ann cups his cheeks with both hands. She stares into the green eyes that suck her into a depth of love she can only have with Mark. "I propose we spend one-month dating and getting to know each other. We might find we don't like each other or discover we do very much. Then, after that month of discovery, if we like each other, we can move to your proposition."

"Dating?" Mark asks quietly as his forehead creases with thought. "Like movies, dinner, dancing? Those kinds of things?"

"Yes, those kinds of things or whatever people our age do on dates these days." Mary Ann shrugs and drops her hands as she sits back on her heels.

Mark stares into the blue-gray eyes he fell in love with so many years ago. He feels as if his heart is going to explode with relief. Mark slides his fingertips over Mary Ann's soft cheek and then her lips as she closes her eyes. He leans over. He kisses her eyelids, the tip of her nose, and finally, her lips gently.

"Thank you, Kitten."

"Is that a yes?"

Mark stands, lifts her, and swings her around. "Yes. Yes. Yes!" he yells at the top of his lungs. "Can we start today?" he asks, setting her on the ground.

Mary Ann giggles like a high school girl. "I don't see why not. Mark, just remember this. You don't have to use your money to impress me. Just be yourself."

"Okay." Mark takes two steps back and eyes Mary Ann from top to bottom. He licks his lips and clears his throat. "Mary Ann, would you like to have dinner with me tonight?"

She looks him over the same way he looked her over. Mary Ann pretends to consider his question. Then she smiles, "only if we can have pizza at the place we stopped last time we drove back to Phoenix."

"We can definitely do that," Mark answers with his 1,000-watt smile.

Mary Ann looks into his eyes and sees nothing but love in those eyes. I don't think I'll last a month, she feels as she takes his hand, and they walk to the parking lot.

Chapter 36

The month passes quickly for Mary Ann. She and Mark talk every day. Because Mark still works, he and Mary Ann agree to go out one night a week and spend weekends together. Mark is the perfect gentleman, always picking Mary Ann up at her house and walking her to her door. Every morning, a red rose is lying on top of Mary Ann's newspaper on her doorstep.

They spend some evenings around Mark's pool, but Mary Ann refuses to sleep at Mark's house. So either he picks her up, or she drives to his house. The couple goes to see movies and the theater. Mary Ann cooks for Mark at her house, and Mark grills at his home. The couple discovers how much they like the older version of themselves and how compatible they are.

Like before, Mark never attempts to get fresh with Mary Ann. Their kisses reflect the passion and desire they feel toward each other, but they refrain from going any further.

On the last day of Mary Ann's proposed dating month, which is a Friday, the couple spends the evening around Mark's pool. Stacy cooked a fabulous dinner for the couple before disappearing for the evening.

Mary Ann lounges in the hot tub while Mark swims several laps around the pool. She watches him climb out of the pool. Her heart feels like it will jump out of her chest, gazing at him. As he dries off and approaches her, Mark provides her his 1,000-watt smile.

"Mark, today is the last day of my thirty-day proposition."

"I know. So how do you feel now about my thirty days?"

Mary Ann starts to climb out of the heated tub, and Mark offers his hand to help her. Once she is out, she looks at him.

"Mark, today is my birthday."

"I know. I planned for us to celebrate tomorrow, depending on today's outcome."

"Mark, I've given a lot of thought to your thirty-day proposition," she says, remembering the words she spoke to him so many years ago. "I've tried to fight these feelings inside me, but I'm tired of fighting them. I want to be yours in every way. That's what I want for my birthday, so we can skip your thirty days if that's okay with you."

"Kitten, are you sure? I would love that very much, but I want you to be sure."

"I am sure, Mark. You are the only man I will ever love. It's time. Please, will you give me that gift?"

Mark stares at Mary Ann for several seconds. Then he says, "I'll be right back." Mary Ann dries off while waiting for Mark to return. When he does, he lifts her into his arms and carries her to his bedroom. Just like before, the room smells of lavender. Lit candles are everywhere, and red rose petals cover the open bed. Mark removes her swimsuit and gently lays Mary Ann on the bed. Then he undresses himself while admiring the beautiful woman he loves.

About Author

Gaylene Nunn is a widowed 60+ year old woman who spent her career in banking, financial services, municipal government, and most recently as CFO for a upper level regional university that she helped create. She retired in 2017 with the title of Vice President Emeritus. Gaylene is a Texas native who enjoys reading, writing, traveling, and spending time with her dog, Sam, and cat, Emily.

Also By

Gaylene Nunn
Before Your Loved Ones Goes — Planning for Your Reality

Deserie LaCrosse & Gaylene Nunn
An Eternity of Love
Damaged by Love

Made in the USA
Middletown, DE
04 March 2023

26030210R00106